Sugar and Spice

The Cupcake Club

Sheryl Berk and Carrie Berk

sourcebooks
jabberwocky

Published by Sourcebooks Jabberwocky, an imprint of Sourcebooks, Inc.
P.O. Box 4410, Naperville, Illinois 60567-4410
(630) 961-3900
Fax: (630) 961-2168
www.sourcebooks.com

Library of Congress Cataloging-in-Publication Data

Berk, Sheryl.
  Sugar and spice / Sheryl Berk and Carrie Berk.
     pages cm. -- (The cupcake club ; [7])
  Summary: When Blakely Elementary's new art teacher, Mr. Dubois, becomes the advisor for Peace, Love, and Cupcakes, his zany ideas irk club founder Kylie, but orders are pouring in so quickly that there is no time to argue, and Lexi is busy competing against school bully Meredith in a pageant.
  (13 : alk. paper) [1. Pageants--Fiction. 2. Clubs--Fiction. 3. Friendship--Fiction. 4. Cupcakes--Fiction. 5. Baking--Fiction.] I. Berk, Carrie. II. Title.
  PZ7.B45236Sug 2015
  [Fic]--dc23

                              2014047378

Source of Production: Versa Press, East Peoria, Illinois, USA
Date of Production: March 2015
Run Number: 5003494

                Printed and bound in the United States of America.
                     VP 10 9 8 7 6 5 4 3 2 1

To Hannah Banana, a.k.a. Hannah Stark
You'll always be my sister! You inspire so many girls to be
strong, and I'm so proud of you!
Forever, Carrie

Accidents Do Happen

With Meredith Mitchell, Blakely Elementary School's resident mean girl, all it took was one little incident to become her instant enemy. Kylie Carson learned this the hard way in third grade when she accidentally kicked a sneaker in Meredith's face during an audition for the hip-hop club. Ever since that black eye, Meredith held a grudge against Kylie and all the other members of her cupcake club: Sadie, Jenna, Lexi, and Delaney.

Somehow, they'd managed to keep the peace through most of fourth, and now fifth, grade. Meredith was annoying, stuck-up, and opinionated, but she paid little attention to them and instead surrounded herself with a posse of worshipping minions—a.k.a. Abby, Emily, and Bella. But this morning, Lexi was innocently carrying her huge art project down the hallway…

"Excuse me. Pardon me," Lexi said as she tried to

navigate her way to first-period art class with a canvas that was bigger than she was. On it, she'd painted a colorful carnival scene: a merry-go-round, a Ferris wheel, and a group of girls (looking a lot like her fellow members of Peace, Love, and Cupcakes) eating cotton candy. It had taken her nearly a week to complete, and she was proud of her work. But now, as she slammed into walls, lockers, and assorted students, she thought maybe she'd gone a little overboard.

"Watch where you're going with that thing!" Jack Yu snapped as Lexi accidentally whacked him in the head with her canvas.

"I'm so sorry!" she apologized. "It's hard to see where I'm going."

"Ouch!" complained Emily Dutter. "You klutz! You stepped on my foot."

"Sorry!" Lexi called after her. "I didn't mean to."

The hall was packed with fifth graders cramming their coats and book bags into their lockers. Lexi tried her best to squeeze past them without doing too much damage. "Heads up! Art project coming through!" she warned. She never saw Meredith applying her pink lipstick by her locker mirror, and the painting collided with the diva's elbow.

"Nooooo!" Meredith shrieked in horror. There was a hot-pink smudge across her mouth and cheek. "Who did this? Who would *dare*?"

She saw the huge canvas only inches away from her locker—but couldn't see who was hiding behind it.

"I said, *Who is responsible for this?*" she bellowed.

Lexi peered around the edge of the painting. "Um, I guess I am?"

Meredith's eyes narrowed. "You! You did this!"

"I'm really, really sorry," Lexi began, but Meredith cut her off.

"Oh, you will be!"

Lexi rested her painting against the wall and dug in her backpack. "Wait, I think I have some tissues in here." She took one out and began dabbing at Meredith's cheek, spreading the color on her nose and chin. Now her whole face looked pink and blotchy.

"Get off me!" Meredith screamed. "You're making it worse!" She snatched the tissue out of Lexi's hand as a crowd gathered around them.

"OMG!" Emily cried. "Meredith, your face is a mess!"

"I dunno." Jack chuckled. "I think it's an improvement."

Lexi braced herself and waited for Meredith to throw a

royal temper tantrum. She wished she could duck behind her painting and take cover—or climb into a locker and shut the door tight. This wasn't going to be pretty.

"How dare you humiliate me?" Meredith hissed at Lexi.

"I didn't mean to. Honest!" she insisted. "It's just makeup. You can wash it off."

"Poor Meredith," Abby cooed, patting her friend on the back. "Your lips were perfectly pink and sparkly."

"I know." Meredith sighed. "Now it's all spoiled. That loser Lexi ruined it!"

Luckily, the first-period bell rang and Principal Fontina came out of her office to see what all of the commotion was about. When she saw a pink-faced Meredith towering over Lexi, she had a hunch.

"Ms. Mitchell," Principal Fontina said, "that bell means you should be in class. Now!"

Meredith slammed the locker shut and gave Lexi one last evil glare. Then she hurried down the hall to Ms. Murphie's English class.

"Do you need help carrying that?" the principal asked, noticing Lexi's giant painting.

"Um, no thanks," Lexi said nervously, hoisting her canvas into her arms. "I've got it." As Principal Fontina turned to go back to her office, Lexi accidentally smacked her in the butt with the painting.

"Oopsie! Sorry!" Lexi said. "My bad."

"Next time, Miss Poole, maybe think a bit smaller," her principal suggested. "I applaud you for your hard work, but I'm worried it's not going to fit through the art room door."

With a little maneuvering, Lexi made her way down the hall and found herself standing at the doorway to Ms. McNalley's studio. Lexi tried to just walk through the door, but the painting was too wide. So she tilted it sideways, stood behind it, and gave it a firm push through the door frame.

"Whoa!" her friend Kylie exclaimed as Lexi and the canvas burst into the room. "That is one humongo art project."

Lexi nodded. "I know. I supersized it."

The rest of the class gathered around, curious, as she peeled away the masking tape and brown paper covering her artwork. There were oohs and ahhs as she revealed the carnival scene.

"Lexi, you outdid yourself. Your painting is breathtaking," Ms. McNalley exclaimed.

Lexi blushed. "Thank you. I tried really hard."

Kylie noticed that her friend wasn't enjoying all the

praise from her peers and teacher. She seemed distracted. "What's up, Lex?" she whispered. "Why the long face?"

"Meredith Mitchell hates my guts." Lexi sighed. "I kinda bumped into her with my painting and messed up her makeup."

Kylie wanted to giggle—she could just picture Meredith's face covered in brightly colored smudges. But she knew this was no laughing matter. Lexi looked worried.

"Did she freak?"

"She had that look in her eye," Lexi told her BFF. "You know, the death stare."

Kylie nodded. She knew it well. "You can't let her get to you," she insisted. "Bullies count on you being scared of them."

"I'm not scared," Lexi said, settling into her drawing desk. "I'm *terrified*. If Ms. Fontina hadn't come along, I think Meredith would have killed me."

Kylie put an arm around her shoulder. "You have me, Jenna, Sadie, and Delaney behind you."

Lexi heaved a sigh of relief. It was great to know her friends had her back. Still, she had a sinking feeling that this wasn't over yet. Not if Meredith had something to say about it.

2

The Wicked Witch of Blakely

That afternoon at lunch, Lexi spotted Meredith carrying her tray to a table with Abby, Bella, and Emily. She quickly ducked behind Jenna, who was waiting in the cafeteria food line.

"*Qué pasa, chica?*" her friend asked. "What's with the disappearing act?"

"Is she gone?" Lexi asked, peeking out behind Jenna.

"Is who gone?"

"Meredith. I don't want her to see me."

Jenna stepped aside. "Do not tell me you're scared of her and her *boca grande!*"

"It's not her big mouth I'm scared of," Lexi insisted. "It's just what she might say with it. Like call me 'Loser Lexi,' for example."

"Sticks and stones," Jenna reminded her. "You can't let her intimidate you. Whenever she used to call me

'Thunder Thighs' or 'Bubble Butt,' I just laughed in her face."

Lexi knew Jenna was right. Still, she couldn't tell her heart to stop pounding every time she caught a glimpse of Meredith anywhere at school.

"I don't know what to do," she confided in her friends at their lunch table. "I apologized, but she didn't seem to care."

"She's such a princess," Sadie weighed in. "She's in my first-period English class, and she spent the whole time in the bathroom reapplying her makeup." Sadie was a tomboy and a star athlete who didn't own a single lip gloss. "So ridiculous!"

"I think you should just forget it ever happened," Kylie added. "Bygones. It's ancient history. Trust me, it's better that way."

Lexi decided that was probably the best idea. It wasn't as if she had *purposely* ruined Meredith's makeup this morning. Surely Meredith had to know that!

"Can we change the topic from bullies to baking?" Kylie suggested. "We received a huge potential order over email this morning."

"Define 'huge,'" Sadie replied. "I have a math final next week and two basketball games."

"And I know Delaney has her school's pep rally on

Friday and is on babysitting duty for her twin brother and sister this weekend," Jenna reminded them.

"That's okay—we have plenty of time," Kylie said, pulling the email printout from her jean jacket pocket. "This order is for six weeks from now."

"Someone likes to plan ahead," Jenna said, peering over Kylie's shoulder. "What's the Miss New England Shooting Starz Pageant?"

"Some kind of talent and runway competition," Kylie replied. "I didn't get a lot of the details. The pageant directors, Laura and Fitzy, want to meet with us and discuss it further. Kind of like an interview."

"How many cupcakes are we talking?" Lexi asked. "A hundred? Two hundred?"

"Try a thousand." Kylie read the letter. "Apparently, they have a huge crowd coming with contestants of all ages—and it's gonna be on TV!"

"TV? Our cupcakes are going to be on TV?" Lexi's mood suddenly brightened. "Now you're talking."

"*If* we get the order," Kylie pointed out. "It appears we're not the only bakers competing for the business. Connecticut Cupcakes is also in the running."

Lexi shuddered to think of the two sisters who had

beaten them on *Battle of the Bakers*. "Well, then we'll just have to prove we're the best," she said. "We'll pull out all the stops. We'll blow them away."

"When do we meet with these pageant peeps?" Sadie asked.

"I told them we were free Sunday morning—and I made sure Delaney could come too. That gives us a few days to brainstorm and make some samples."

Lexi nodded. "I'll sketch out a few designs tonight."

"And I'll go through our recipe file with Jenna," Kylie added. She took a big bite out of her pizza slice. "We've got this!"

☆ ☮ ☆

By the end of the day, Lexi had almost forgotten about the morning's fireworks. When Meredith waltzed into last-period study hall, Lexi simply took her friends' advice and ignored her.

But Meredith wasn't about to forgive and forget so easily. She slid into an empty seat next to Lexi in the back of the classroom. "Your outfit is pretty decent for a change," Meredith whispered to her.

Lexi smiled cautiously. "Thanks?" she replied. Maybe Meredith was trying to be nice for once. Maybe she realized she had overreacted.

"Except for that sweater. It's hideous," Meredith continued. "But it suits you. I wouldn't change a thing."

Emily Dutter, who was also in study hall, snickered. "Meredith, you are *too* funny!"

Ms. Rathbane, the study hall teacher, was busy at her desk grading papers. Lexi considered raising her hand and ratting them both out, but she knew that would only make things worse. So she just sat there, stone-faced, and took it.

"Do you know what I heard?" Meredith asked Emily. "I heard Jeremy Saperstone likes me and is going to ask me out."

"No way!" Emily replied. "Doesn't he have a girlfriend?"

Lexi fumed. They both knew that Jeremy had been *her* boyfriend ever since they'd played Romeo and Juliet in the fifth-grade play.

Meredith wrinkled her nose. "I guess he's dating some loser. For now."

That was it! Lexi couldn't take it anymore. She leaned over and whispered to Meredith, "Jeremy is my boyfriend, and you know it!"

"Why would he want to be with you when he could be with me? I mean, seriously. Just look at me…" Meredith pointed to her stylish, red-leather jacket and matching miniskirt and tossed her flowing blond curls. "And look at *you*."

Lexi knew her ponytail was limp and her purple cardigan had orange stains on it from art class.

"Oh, Meredith, you and Jeremy will make the cutest couple," Emily cooed.

Lexi didn't want to get in trouble with Ms. Rathbane, so she tried to ignore Meredith's and Emily's whispering and focus on her science homework. She noticed that Meredith was doodling hearts on her binder cover with the initials "J.S. + M.M." Lexi gritted her teeth and waited for the bell to ring.

When class was over, she raced out the door to find Jeremy before his chess club meeting started. She stopped by Mr. Danenburn's science lab, but Jeremy wasn't there. Nor was he at his locker or in the library. She finally spotted him coming down the hall with Jack and waved. But before she could reach him, Meredith jumped out and stopped the boys in their tracks.

"Jeremy," she said, flirting with him. "Can I talk to you a sec?"

Jack checked his watch. "That was a sec. You're done, Meredith."

"Zip it," Meredith replied, turning back to Jeremy and batting her eyelashes.

Jeremy rolled his eyes. "I guess. What's up, Meredith?"

"So, I happen to have these awesome VIP tickets to the Eastern Chess Congress in Stamford this weekend."

Jeremy's eyes grew wide. "Are you kidding me? That is like the World Series of chess tournaments! All the greats will be there playing."

Meredith batted her eyelashes. "I know. And I'm, like, *so* into chess."

Jeremy stared. "You are? I would think a girl like you would hate chess."

"OMG! I love it! There's a queen in the game, isn't there?" She cut him off before he could say another word.

"So you'll come, right? It's a date."

Jeremy shrugged. "Sure. I mean, I can't pass up the Eastern Chess Congress, can I?"

"Great! I'll pick you up at 10:00 a.m. sharp on Sunday. Can't wait!" She blew him a kiss and skipped off.

Lexi stood a few feet away, stunned. She walked up to Jeremy with tears in her eyes.

"How could you?" she asked him. "How could you dump me for the Wicked Witch of Blakely?"

"What? Lex, I'm not dumping you. She just asked me to go to a chess tournament. It's no biggie."

"But it is," Lexi insisted. "Meredith is trying to steal you away from me—and I guess she succeeded."

"You're acting crazy," Jeremy told her. "I'm not dating Meredith!"

"Now you think I'm crazy?" Lexi cried. "What else did Meredith tell you about me?"

"She didn't tell me anything. You're the one who's making a scene in the hallway."

Lexi looked around. Many other students were staring at them and whispering.

"Great. Now everyone knows we broke up," she said, sniffling.

"We didn't break up!" Jeremy tried to convince her. "Unless that's what you want."

Lexi shook her head. She didn't know what she wanted at this moment. Her whole world felt like it was crashing down around her.

"I just want to be left alone," she said, pushing through the crowd and running down the hall.

Kylie caught the end of the argument and called after her. "Lexi! Wait!" She looked at Jeremy, who was equally confused. "What happened?"

"If you figure it out, let me know," he said, sighing.

3

Hangin' with Herbie

When Kylie tried calling Lexi on her cell phone that night, it went straight to voice mail: "You've reached Lexi—leave a message!" So Kylie left several messages, but her friend never returned them. She tried texting and even direct messaging Lexi on Instagram. As Jenna would say, "Nada."

"It isn't like her to ignore my calls," she told Jenna and Sadie at school the next morning. "I'm worried."

"She wasn't in English either," Sadie added. "Maybe she's home sick."

"Or trying to escape the evil clutches of Monster Meredith," Kylie pointed out. "We have to do something."

Sadie checked her basketball schedule. "We could go over to her house after school. I can let Delaney know we're moving the PLC meeting there instead of in the Blakely teachers' lounge."

Kylie nodded. "I better let Herbie know too." Their

beloved cupcake club advisor Juliette was now off in London, married and playing the role of a maid on the British TV show *Downton Abbey*. She'd suggested that her younger brother, Herbie, who'd just graduated from college in Canada, take over for her and help the girls out. But Herbie was no Juliette—while she taught drama, he was a nerdy robotics genius who didn't know a whisk from a spatula.

"I promise you, I am a very quick study," he'd told them. "And I have some keen ideas on how to maximize PLC's potential as a business."

Kylie didn't like Herbie for several reasons: (1) he was a guy; (2) he knew more about monster movies than she did; and (3) he used the word "keen" in practically every sentence. Who did that?

But they were stuck with him and had to make the best of it. Juliette wasn't coming back, and PLC needed an advisor to stay in business. So Herbie would have to do.

Kylie found him in the Blakely robotics lab working on what looked like a deflated beach ball with a long hose attached. Jeremy and Jack had him for their robotics elective and said he was pretty amazing with computers and machines. But Kylie just thought he was weird.

"What is that thing?" she asked.

Herbie pulled off his safety goggles and placed them on top of his shaggy red hair.

"I'm so glad you asked, Kylie," he replied. "This is my idea for speeding up our PLC cleanup."

"We don't bake in the sand or a swimming pool," Kylie corrected him. "What's with the beach ball?"

"I call this the flour-nator," he explained. "Although it will work just as well for sugar, baking powder, salt— whatever other dry ingredients you girls manage to scatter all over the kitchen floor." He flipped a switch and the ball filled with air. "Hand me that sack of flour over there."

Kylie carried over a two-pound bag, and Herbie dumped the entire contents on one of the worktables.

"What are you doing?" she asked, watching a cloud of white dust rise in the air. "You're making a huge mess."

"Exactly," Herbie replied. "Now watch how easily I clean it up."

He waved the hose in the air and the white cloud disappeared into the beach ball. The mountain of flour on the table did the same in seconds.

"Wow, that's pretty cool," Kylie admitted. "That hose has a lot of power."

Suddenly the lights in the robotics lab went off. Then the lights in the hallway. Then the lights on the entire first floor.

"Maybe a little too much power," Herbie said, his cheeks flushing red. "I think I just blew a fuse. Again."

Mr. Mullivan, the chief custodian, walked into the room. "Mr. Dubois, what did I tell you about maxing out the voltage?" he asked, sighing. "Every time those lights go out, I know who's responsible." He took his tools from his belt and started poking around in the power box on the wall. In seconds, the lights came back on.

"Thank you," Herbie replied. "I'll make some adjustments."

"Please do," Mr. Mullivan said sternly. "Every time I see you with those safety goggles on, I get nervous."

"Were you looking for me for a reason?" Herbie asked Kylie as he tinkered with the flour-nator motor.

"Oh yeah. I almost forgot. We're having our meeting at Lexi's house today after school—although she doesn't know it."

Herbie wrinkled his brow. "And why doesn't she know it? Are we surprising her with a PLC meeting?"

"Sorta," Kylie answered. "She's not answering my calls."

"So you believe that ambushing her is the best strategy," Herbie said. "I'm not sure I'm keen on that."

There was that "keen" word again! "You might not be keen on it, but I know my BFF," Kylie insisted. "Sometimes Lex just needs a little push."

"You know, when I was a young, my sister thought she could push me around." Herbie continued twisting wires with a pair of pliers. "I was shy and quiet, and Juliette was bossy."

Kylie sighed. "I don't see what this has to do with Lexi."

"I'm just saying sometimes people don't like to be pushed. They need time to figure things out for themselves."

Kylie gathered up her backpack, ignoring his advice. "So three forty-five at 11 Candlewood Lane, right off Frisbee Street," she said. "See ya."

☆ ☮ ☆

When they arrived at Lexi's, she was curled up on the couch in her pj's. Her mom let them in as Lexi hid under a throw blanket.

"I like the little rainbow unicorns on your jammies," Delaney teased her, noting the flannel pant legs that were poking out.

"Go ahead. Make fun of my clothes. Meredith already did that," Lexi said, still buried under the throw.

"Let's not say the *M* word, shall we?" Kylie suggested, pushing her way into the living room with a bag of groceries and the PLC recipe binder.

Herbie waved his finger in her face. "Uh, uh, uh. Remember what I said about being pushy."

"I feel sick," Lexi said. "Please go. I don't feel like meeting today. Maybe you guys can go to Kylie's instead."

"Nope! We're all here and I officially call this meeting to order," Kylie insisted, yanking the blanket off Lexi and tossing a few pillows on the floor. "Everyone take a seat."

"So I won't mention M.M., but what did I miss?" Delaney asked the group. "I don't go to Blakely, remember—I'm at Weber Day. You gotta fill me in on the drama."

"Me too," Herbie added. "Why are you in a funk, Lexi?"

"A funk? I'm not in a funk," Lexi insisted. "I am destroyed. My life is ruined."

"Ah, I see," Herbie said, taking notes on his iPad. "Is that all?"

Lexi sat up. "Meredith Mitchell hates my guts—and she stole my Jeremy."

Delaney shook her head. "And you let her? Lex, have you learned nothing from being a member of PLC?"

"That's right," Jenna pointed out. "We thought you were done being shy Lexi."

"I was. I mean, I am," Lexi said. "It's just that around Meredith, I forget. With all of you, I'm confident. But Meredith makes me feel—"

"Wonky," Herbie suggested.

"Well, I wouldn't quite put it that way," Lexi replied.

"I would. When my robot is acting wonky, he's out of sorts. He's teetering about and he's not himself. Sometimes he'll even topple over."

Lexi mulled it over. "Okay, so let's say Meredith makes me feel *wonky*. How do I fix it?"

"The same way I fix my robot. I reinforce him so he's not wobbling or off balance anymore." He motioned to Sadie, Jenna, Kylie, and Delaney. "I'd say this crew is your reinforcement."

"We told you we have your back," Kylie reminded her. "We can stand up to Meredith."

"And I can keep an eye on Jeremy," Jenna pointed out. "He's in three of my classes. If Meredith tries to get too close to him, I'll sit on her and squash her like a bug."

Lexi laughed at the image. "Okay, I guess I could try. I don't think my mom was going to let me stay home from school another day anyway."

Dr. Poole called in from the kitchen. "You bet I wasn't! I have real sick pets in the veterinary clinic to tend to."

Kylie held up her binder. "Can we get back to business?"

Lexi smiled. "I'm feeling less wonky already."

4

Something's Fishy

Kylie pulled out an order form. "This came in last night, and it's a rush for tomorrow," she said, handing it to Lexi. "I thought it could be a really fun decorating job for you."

"Six dozen sushi-themed cupcakes for a birthday party at Bridgeport Teppanyaki Palace," Lexi read aloud.

"What's teppan-yucki?" Delaney asked.

"Teppan-*yah*-ki," Lexi corrected her. "It's a Japanese meal that the chef grills right in front of you on a table. My Aunt Dee took me once in New York City."

Delaney nodded. "Cool. Like barbecue."

"Kinda," Kylie added. "But no burgers or hot dogs—more like chicken, meat, fish, and veggies cut into little pieces."

Delaney stared at the order form. "They want cupcakes with fondant sushi on them? Eel, shrimp, and raw tuna? Eww!"

"It could be worse," Herbie reminded them. "They could have asked us to put *real* raw fish on top."

Lexi wrinkled her nose. "Are you sure we can't talk this client into some pretty cupcakes with Japanese cherry blossoms on them?"

Kylie pointed to the note in all-capital letters: "AUTHENTIC-LOOKING SUSHI ROLLS ON EACH CUPCAKE."

Jenna patted Lexi on the back. "You sketch and give me a little time to get my taste buds tuned up," she said.

"No soy sauce or wasabi in the batter," Kylie warned her.

"Or those little orange fish eggs," Herbie chimed in. "I say no to roe!"

Kylie rolled her eyes. "Just leave the cupcakes to us," she dictated. "We got this."

☆ ☮ ☆

Three hours later, what they had was a mess in the kitchen. Lexi's fondant sushi toppers all looked realistic—especially the eel airbrushed to look slimy. But they couldn't agree on the kind of cake or frosting. Everything they tried tasted strange.

"Would it be too gross to do a shrimp-flavored icing?" Delaney asked.

Jenna pretended to gag. "Uh, *sí*. Sugar and shrimp do not mix."

"I guess that rules out soy-sauce flavor too," Sadie said.

"Wasn't the batch of wasabi cupcakes bad enough?" Jenna groaned.

"I think we need to steer clear of all things sushi," Herbie suggested. "What else do you think of when you think of Japanese cuisine?"

"Mochi ice cream," Lexi said. "You know, those cute little round, pounded rice treats?"

"Mochi would melt if we put it inside a cupcake," Sadie pointed out.

"Okay, but it's a step in the right direction," Herbie said, scratching his head. "What else?"

"Green tea!" Kylie suddenly shouted. "A green tea cupcake would be delicious. I've had green tea crepes and macaroons, and they're amazing."

"And we could do a green tea buttercream," Jenna added, smacking her lips together. "I think that would work, and the green color would be beautiful."

She scribbled a shopping list on a piece of paper and handed it to Herbie. "We'll need matcha powder from the gourmet grocery."

"Matcha whatta?" Herbie asked.

"*Aye, dios mío!*" Jenna exclaimed. "It's green tea powder."

"Gotcha—I mean matcha!" Herbie teased. "Back in a jiffy."

When their advisor was gone, Kylie seized the moment to talk about their upcoming "competition" against Connecticut Cupcakes for the pageant job.

"They're pros with tons of experience—not to mention several cookbooks, a dozen stores, and their own line of designer aprons! Of course the pageant will hire them over us," Delaney said.

"Not so fast," Kylie replied. "We can out-bake them. We just have to be smart about it."

Lexi pulled out her sketchbook. "At first I was thinking about rock-candy jewels, but I realized pageants have amazing crowns. I think we should do a tower of cupcakes with a life-sized, pulled-sugar tiara on top."

"Whoa!" Sadie exclaimed. "You've been watching the Food Channel way too much, Lex. We're not sugar artists."

"But we're cupcake artists," Kylie insisted. "We can figure anything out if we set our minds to it. I think we should hear Lexi out. How big a tower were you thinking?"

She held her hand way above her head. "Six, maybe seven feet high, with scalloped edges like the peaks of the crown."

Kylie studied the drawing carefully. "What if we did

mirrored shelves for each level—when I think beauty, I think of looking in a mirror, don't you?"

Now it was Jenna's turn to speak up. "I know we were talking about a vanilla cupcake, but that seemed so ordinary," she said. "What do you guys think of devil's food with chocolate ganache? Something rich and decadent to go with our dazzling sugar crown."

"I think my mouth is watering," Delaney said. "That sounds yummy."

"What do you think Connecticut Cupcakes will make?" Kylie asked. "They've got some pretty original flavors in their stores. Last month's was black pepper chocolate."

Jenna made a face. "What beauty queen would want to eat black pepper chocolate?" she asked. "I'm telling you, our idea is way better."

"Let's hope so," Kylie said. "Miss New England Shooting Starz could make stars out of PLC. We just need to get them to hire us."

5

Crowning Touch

Kylie's mom dropped them off at the building that housed Miss New England Shooting Starz. It was a plain, white-brick structure with not a hint of glamour or glitz—just lots and lots of offices.

"Which door do you suppose is Starz's?" Lexi asked.

Kylie pointed down a hallway where a long, pink carpet was laid out. "I'd say it's the one at the end of that."

They knocked on the door, and a pretty, perky assistant answered. Her long, sandy-blond hair was pulled back in a sleek ponytail, and she was wearing a casual T-shirt and denim miniskirt.

"*You* work for the pageant?" Delaney asked.

"I do," the young woman replied. "What were you expecting?"

Delaney shrugged. "I kinda thought you might be wearing an evening gown and a tiara."

The woman laughed. "Nah, I save the crown for the weekend," she said with a wink. "My name is Hershey."

Jenna looked puzzled. "As in the chocolate bar? Or the kiss?"

"As in Elsabeth Hershey. Everyone just calls me Hershey for short."

"Why don't they call you Elsa for short?" Sadie suggested.

"And deal with all the *Frozen* jokes? No thanks!" Hershey replied. "I'd rather be a candy bar."

"Me too!" Jenna exclaimed. "Although a Double Stuf Oreo would be my top choice."

"We're Peace, Love, and Cupcakes." Kylie stepped in, trying to steer the conversation back to the reason why they were there. "We have some cupcakes for the pageant directors to sample."

Hershey's eyes lit up. "Cupcakes? You brought cupcakes? What kind?"

"It's kind of a surprise," Lexi said, placing the box behind her back. "We don't want to give it away."

Hershey nodded. "I gotcha. I'll go see if I can find Laura and Fitzy. It's always crazy here the month before the pageant. So much to do and prepare, ya know?"

Lexi shrugged. "Nope, I don't know. But it sounds cool."

"It is! We have more than two hundred girls competing from all over the country."

She disappeared in the back of the office while the girls made themselves at home on a big, pink couch.

"Check it out," Jenna said, pointing to a huge, glittering rhinestone crown on a shelf. "I'd look good in that, don't you think?"

"I think it would give me a headache," Lexi said, sighing. "It probably weighs a ton."

Jenna jumped off the couch. "Well, let's find out!"

She gently took the crown off the shelf. "You're right. It *is* heavy," she said. She placed it on her head and spun around. "How do I look? *Muy bonita?*"

"You look like Glinda from *The Wizard of Oz*," Delaney said, giggling.

Jenna did her best royal wave. "I could get used to this." Then she plunked the crown on Delaney's head.

"Here she is…Miss Peace, Love, and Cupcakes," Delaney crooned, pretending to walk an imaginary runway.

"Come on, Delaney," Lexi fretted. "Put it back before we get in trouble."

"Not until you try it on," Delaney insisted. She placed the crown on Lexi's head and stepped back to admire it.

"Whoa! Lex, you look *como una reina*—like a queen," Jenna said, whistling through her teeth.

"I feel silly," Lexi replied, snatching it off. "I'm not a pageant queen."

"But you could be," said a voice entering the room. It was Laura, the pageant director. "All you need is the confidence to be a star."

Lexi's cheeks flushed bright red. "I'm so sorry!" she apologized, handing the crown back to Laura. "We were just trying it on for size."

"No worries!" the director replied. "This was my crown from when I was Miss New England Shooting Starz twenty years ago. I was Ultimate Grand Supreme."

"Is that, like, the best?" Delaney asked.

"Well, it's the top prize," Laura explained. "But there are lots of other categories as well, like prettiest smile, best personality, ultimate talent…"

It was easy to see why Laura had won. She had warm, brown eyes; silky, brown hair that fell in loose ringlets around her shoulders; and perfect, white teeth. And unlike Hershey, she was dressed to the nines in a pale-blue suit and high heels.

"Is there a category for most baskets in a single game?" Sadie asked. "I'd win that for sure."

"Afraid not," Laura said, smiling. "But there is a fitness category where you can show off your sports skill."

"You could dribble your ball onstage," Delaney teased, elbowing Sadie. "Or do an ollie on your skateboard."

"Well, if there was a category for best cupcake, PLC would win it," Kylie said, motioning for Lexi to bring over the samples. "I hope you like what we created for your pageant."

"Did I hear the word 'cupcake'?" A bubbly, blond woman suddenly bounced into the room. She was dressed head to toe in pink, from her fuchsia beanie with "STAR" on it to her pink sweater, leggings, and bubble-gum pink patent-leather boots. She was carrying several sequined gowns, draped over both arms.

"I'm Fitzy. And you are?"

"Speechless," Delaney replied. "Those are the most gorgeous dresses I've ever seen!"

"Ya think?" Fitzy asked. "I can't decide if this is fab or drab." She held up an emerald-green dress with fringe on the bottom.

Delaney gasped. "OMG! It's amazing!"

"I agree—if you're a leprechaun," Laura sniffed.

"Or a pistachio nut," Jenna spoke up. "Just sayin'."

Laura looked up from her clipboard. "I like this girl. She's got style."

Jenna looked down at her gray sweatshirt, jeans, and black high-top sneakers. "Really? 'Cause these are just my sisters' hand-me-downs."

"Style isn't just what you wear on the outside. It's what you project from the inside," Fitzy explained. "Confidence is your best accessory."

"Phew," Jenna said, mopping her brow. "That's a relief."

"That's what our pageant's all about," Laura added. "Celebrating girls who are beautiful inside and out. Do you think you could come up with a cupcake that embodies that?"

Lexi held open the box. "We made these sparkling spun-sugar crown toppers."

Fitzy handed Sadie her pile of clothes. "Hold this. I need a closer taste—I mean, look."

Both directors examined the cupcakes. They looked them over from every angle and sampled the cake and the frosting individually, then together.

"They are certainly works of art," Laura commented.

Fitzy licked her fingertips. "And scrumptious!" she said with her mouth full.

"Yummo with a capital *Y*," Hershey weighed in.

Laura tapped a high-heeled pump on the floor. "They really are very good…"

"Good? They're great!" Jenna insisted. "We're talking the finest Belgian chocolate, Madagascar vanilla, and French butter."

"That sounds very worldly," Laura continued. "It's just…"

Lexi sensed there was something that the Starz director was hesitating to tell them.

"We're not hired, are we?" she said quietly.

"I'm sorry," Laura finally answered. "They're just not exactly what we were looking for."

"We can fix it!" Kylie insisted. "You have to give us another crack at it!"

"If you want a second chance, you'll need to be back here with a new batch by 2:00 p.m.," Laura said. "That's when we're expecting Connecticut Cupcakes as well, and we need to make a decision."

Lexi's heart sank. The last time they'd gone head-to-head with the Connecticut Cupcakes sisters, things hadn't turned out well. They had been out-baked, out-decorated, and out-displayed—and had lost the *Battle of the Bakers* in front of millions of TV viewers. She shuddered at the thought.

Jenna was more concerned about time. "Um, Kylie, that gives us just three hours to come up with a new recipe, test it, bake it, and decorate. *No es posible!*"

Kylie pushed her toward the door and motioned for the other girls to follow. "Thanks!" she said, waving to the directors. "We'll be back in a jiffy."

"A jiffy? Did you actually say we'd be back in a jiffy?" Lexi groaned as they started hunting through the cabinets in Kylie's kitchen. "I have no idea how we're going to bake and decorate these cupcakes. This could take us days to come up with—not a jiffy!"

"I'm not even sure how long a jiffy is," Delaney admitted.

"It doesn't matter. We just need to focus," Kylie replied. "Somebody toss out some ideas."

"The pageant lady said it's just as important to be beautiful on the inside as it is on the outside," Delaney suggested. "So maybe that's what our cupcake needs to be."

Kylie raised an eyebrow. "Okay, I like where you're going with this."

"Where *are* you going with this?" Sadie asked.

"I'm just saying it would be cool if we could stuff the cupcakes with something pretty," Delaney explained.

Lexi's eyes lit up. "Like a cupcake inside a cupcake!"

"That's brilliant!" Kylie shouted. "We could bake a mini cake and put it *inside* the cupcake. So when you bite in…"

"It's beautiful. Oh, I love it," Lexi said.

"Talk to me about flavors, Jenna," Kylie said. "Something special. Something different…"

"Something pink," Delaney weighed in. "Like that pink outfit Fitzy had on."

Jenna tapped a finger to her chin. "We could do a pink velvet and bake a mini white cake inside. Maybe in a star shape for Miss New England Shooting Starz."

"How do we do that?" Sadie asked. "We've never done a shape inside a cupcake before."

"Easy-peasy," Kylie said, flipping through her recipe collection. "I saw something like this before and wanted to try it." She held up a page. "We bake the white cake first and use a mini cookie cutter to make the stars. Then we put them in the pink velvet batter and they bake right inside the cupcakes."

"What do we think of white chocolate buttercream?" Jenna asked, smacking her lips together. She did her best Fitzy impression: "Is it fab…or drab? Yum…or hum-drum?"

"*Yum!*" the girls shouted unanimously.

"Let's keep it simple on top," Lexi added. "Gold-fondant stars sprinkled with luster dust. Beautiful and elegant, just like a pageant queen."

"I think we've got a plan," Kylie said, climbing a step stool to retrieve the food coloring from the top shelf of the cupboard.

"I bet Connecticut Cupcakes has a plan too," Delaney reminded them. "And a good one."

"Not as good as ours," Kylie insisted. "Laura and Fitzy are gonna love this." She opened the fridge and handed a dozen eggs to Sadie.

"I can take a hint," Sadie said, tying an apron around her waist. "It's time to get cracking!"

☆ ✌ ☆

When Kylie's mom dropped the girls off at the pageant office, a big, pink truck with the letters *CC* on it was already parked in front.

"Connecticut Cupcakes," Kylie said with a sigh. "They beat us to it."

"Of course they did," Sadie grumped. "And they always have to make an entrance." She pointed to a large box on wheels that two bakery assistants were rolling up the walkway.

"What do you suppose is in there?" Lexi asked. "I hate surprises. I'd rather know what we're going up against."

"A ten-ton cupcake?" Delaney guessed.

"Well, there's only one way to find out," Jenna said. "Follow my lead, guys…"

She ran up to the two men dressed in white aprons. They were trying desperately to roll the box over the curb.

"*Hola!*" Jenna said sweetly. "*Habla usted español?*"

The workers stopped and stared. "Um, no, sorry. Only English."

Jenna continued, "*Estoy perdido. Dónde está Holly Lane?*"

"I think she's lost," one worker said to the other. "Go straight for about two blocks, then take a left. At the stop sign, make a right. Then an immediate left at the Sunoco station. That's Holly Lane."

Jenna shrugged. "*No comprendo.*"

"Well, sorry. We can't help you. Our bosses are in there having a meeting, and we gotta get this thing inside."

"*Waaaaah!*" Delaney suddenly ran up behind Jenna, pretending to cry hysterically. She sobbed on her friend's shoulder.

"Okay, okay! Don't cry!" The first worker wiped his

brow with a handkerchief. "We'll help you get where you're going."

"*Muchas gracias!*" Jenna said, shaking his hand.

The workers left the box at the curb and went back to the truck to get a map out of the glove compartment. While Jenna and Delaney distracted them, Kylie, Sadie, and Lexi snuck behind the box. "The sides are all taped shut!" Lexi whispered.

"Sadie, you're tall. Crack open the lid and peek inside."

Sadie stood on her tiptoes—the box was almost six feet tall!

"Well? What do you see?" Kylie whispered.

Sadie's eyes grew wide. "It can't be."

"What? What?" Lexi asked frantically. "What is it?"

"It's a gown," Sadie replied. "A gown made entirely of mini cupcakes."

"No way," Kylie exclaimed. "We made a dozen cupcakes with stars in them, and they made a pageant gown?"

"Worse. It's bright pink," Sadie replied. "Fitzy is gonna love it. We don't stand a chance." She noticed that Delaney was waving them off.

"Quick! We gotta get out of here," Sadie said, grabbing Kylie and Lexi and ducking behind a tree.

The workers returned and hoisted the box over the curb, rolling it up to the office entrance.

Jenna studied Kylie, Sadie, and Lexi's long faces. "That bad?"

"Worse," Lexi said. "They made a huge presentation—a pageant gown made of cupcakes! We'll embarrass ourselves if we show Laura and Fitzy what we made."

"I agree with Lex," Kylie said. "I don't think we can go in there."

Jenna shook her head. "Remember what Laura said: it's not always appearances that count. I say we do it. We're here anyway…"

"Okay," Kylie relented. "But I have an awful feeling about this."

Sibling Rivalry

This time, when Hershey greeted them at the door, she looked a little frazzled. Her hair was tousled, and she seemed out of breath.

"Oh, hi, guys," she said. "You might want to think twice about coming in right this second…"

Kylie heard shouting from the office and the sound of something crashing. "Is everything okay, Hershey?" she asked.

"Kinda," Hershey replied. "Well, not really. The Connecticut Cupcakes sisters are having a bit of a brouhaha."

"What's a broo-ha-ha?" Delaney asked. "Is that like a party? Can we come?"

"It's an argument, and I'm not surprised," Lexi said, recalling how the two had feuded with each other at *Battle of the Bakers*. "Cece and Chloe really push each other's buttons."

"Oh, you know them? Maybe you could come in and

help me referee," Hershey said, taking Lexi by the arm. "I'd appreciate it. They're scaring me."

Lexi peeked in the office. There were the two cupcake sisters, chasing each other around the room.

"I told you this was an awful idea," Chloe said, complaining. "But do you ever listen? *Noooooo!*"

Cece threw a couch pillow at her sister's head. "It was a brilliant idea—until you forgot to top the mini cupcakes with edible pearls like we discussed. You ruined my display."

"I had errands to run," Chloe insisted. "I thought you would handle it."

"Ladies! Ladies!" Hershey held up her hand. "I'm sure it's fine. Laura and Fitzy will be out in a sec if you'll just take a seat."

Cece and Chloe ignored her and kept right on fighting.

"Errands? What errands? Honestly, all you think about is shopping," Cece said, criticizing her younger sister. "You forget we're running a business."

"I'm leaving you in charge while I go get the directors," Hershey told Lexi. "Be careful!"

Lexi just stood there. She had no idea what to do or say to make the pair stop arguing. They reminded her of two little girls squabbling over a toy in the sandbox.

She glanced over at her fellow cupcake clubbers and mouthed the words "Help me."

"Hey! *Escuchen!*" Jenna came to her rescue. The sisters stopped and stared. "Listen up! You two need to cool it!"

"Yeah," Lexi said, trying to calm them down. "Your cupcake gown rocks. You both did an amazing job, so just stop fighting about it."

Cece looked shocked. "How do you know we made a cupcake gown? It's all boxed up. You better not have touched it…"

"Um, she means she can *imagine* how gorgeous it is." Kylie tried to cover for her friend. "Lexi has a very vivid imagination."

"But how did you know we made a gown?" Chloe asked. "We never told you that."

"She's psychic," Delaney piped up. "She reads palms and crystal balls and stuff."

Chloe's mouth fell open. "Seriously? You see the future?"

"I guess," Lexi said, blushing. "I mean, sure."

Chloe stuck her palm under Lexi's nose. "Can you tell my future? Is my boyfriend finally going to pop the question over dinner tonight?"

Lexi hemmed and hawed. "Well, it might possibly happen definitely."

"I told you! I told you!" Chloe started jumping up and down. Then she hugged Lexi. "This is the best news! I have to go out and buy a new outfit for the proposal."

Cece looked even madder. "You are *not* going shopping. We have a dozen orders due tomorrow."

Chloe picked up her purse and waved. "Toodles! Misters before sisters!" And just like that, she swept out the door.

"One down, one to go," Sadie whispered to Lexi. "Good job!"

"Well, who needs her?" Cece sniffed. "I can make the presentation by myself."

When Laura and Fitzy reappeared, she introduced herself and unveiled her cupcake display. "Impressive, don't you think?" she asked the directors. "It's a gown made entirely out of cupcakes!"

Fitzy circled around and around the display, admiring it from every angle. "It's certainly large. And it really looks like something you'd see on a pageant runway."

"I knew you'd love it. So I'll send you my invoice in the a.m. and we can get working on the real display for your pageant."

"Just a second!" Kylie protested. "We get a turn to show our cupcakes too. We baked a whole second batch."

Cece looked down at the small, white box Lexi was holding and snickered. "That's your presentation? Pullease!"

Lexi opened it and took out a single cupcake. She handed it to Laura. "It represents everything you asked for. It's beautiful inside and out," she explained.

Laura took a bite…and beamed. "Is that a star I see? Right inside the cupcake?"

"It is," Kylie said proudly. Then she shot Cece a look. "Impressive. Don't you think?"

"I think the cupcake gown will definitely make a statement," Fitzy said. "Fashion and frosting. How can you go wrong?"

"True," Laura said. "But Peace, Love, and Cupcakes *did* listen to what we asked for and gave us exactly what we wanted."

She turned to Cece. "I'm so sorry, but we're going to go with them this time around."

"No!" Cece stomped her foot and pouted. "It's all Chloe's fault. This silly cupcake gown was all her idea."

"I thought it was your idea," Sadie responded. "Isn't that what you said?"

This time it was Cece's turn to grab her purse and bolt out the door.

"I see big disappointment in her future," Lexi said, pretending to have a vision. "And a big pageant order in ours!"

8

Runway Rival

The girls were piling back into Kylie's mom's SUV when a black Cadillac suddenly whizzed by them. It pulled right up to the Miss New England Shooting Starz office. Kylie rolled down the window of the passenger seat to get a better look—and spotted a familiar figure stepping out. Meredith!

She quickly rolled up the window and tried to hide her panic from her friends.

"What's wrong, honey?" her mom asked, noticing Kylie's face turn pale. "You look queasy."

"Um, nah. I'm okay," Kylie replied, unbuckling her seat belt. "I just realized I left my phone in the pageant office. Be back in a jiffy!" She opened the door and raced back out.

"There she goes with the jiffy thing again," Delaney said.

"She would forget her head if it wasn't pinned on her shoulders," her mom teased.

Kylie ran into the building and stood right outside the

Starz office door. It was open a crack, and she could just make out the conversation.

"You must be Meredith Mitchell," she heard Hershey saying. "So lovely to meet you."

"Of course it is!" Meredith replied. "And this is my pageant coach."

Kylie pushed the door open a tad more to get a peek at the coach. A woman in a bright-red coat offered Hershey her hand and Meredith's portfolio. "I'm Jennifer Amaryllis, like the flower."

"Nice to meet you Miss Flower…I mean, Miss Amaryllis," Hershey said.

"Please. Call me Miss Jen."

"Well, Miss Jen, we're happy to have Meredith join us as a contestant in the Miss New England Shooting Starz pageant. I trust all your paperwork is complete?"

Miss Jen handed her a folder. "Of course it is. I know what I'm doing," she insisted. "I've had two of my girls go on to compete in Miss America. No one I coach loses."

"Great." Hershey smiled politely. "Then best of luck, and we'll see you in a few weeks."

"Just one question," the coach said, interrupting her. "Meredith has many talents but wants to do an extreme baton-twirling routine and tap dance. How high are the ceilings in the hotel ballroom?"

"I will definitely check," Hershey replied, ushering them to the door. "So nice of you stop by."

Kylie ran back to the car and jumped inside, just minutes before Meredith and Miss Jen made their departure from Starz.

"Did you get it?" Lexi asked, as Kylie slammed the passenger door.

"Get what?"

"Your cell phone, silly!" her mom said. "Remember? You left in the pageant office?"

"Oh! I found it in my back pocket. Whoopsie!"

"Kylie Carson," her mom said, laughing as they drove off. "What am I going to do with you?"

But all Kylie was thinking was, "What am I going to do about Meredith?"

☆ ☮ ☆

When the girls went to Delaney's house the next day to talk over the pageant order plans, their cupcake club president was strangely quiet.

"*Qué pasa, chica?*" Jenna asked her. "You seem a little out of it."

"I'm just thinking," Kylie said, sighing.

"Thinking about what?" Lexi questioned. "How we're going to make all those pageant cupcakes and a giant tower? Don't worry. It's under control."

"My dad said he'd help us build the display," Sadie said.

"No, it's not that," Kylie said.

"Then what?" Jenna pushed. "We're your friends. You can tell us."

Kylie took a deep breath. "When I went back to the pageant office, it wasn't to get my phone. I saw something."

"What do you mean you saw something?" Sadie said. "Something cool?"

"No," Kylie said. "Something that tied my stomach all up in knots."

"A monster?" Delaney giggled. "Vampire or zombie?"

"Worse," Kylie answered. "The meanest monster you could ever encounter."

Lexi felt a chill go down her spine. "Meredith."

Kylie nodded. "I saw her pull up to the pageant office and I kinda eavesdropped."

"And?" Lexi asked, shaking Kylie by the shoulders. "What did you find out? Was she trying to sabotage our business?"

"Not exactly. She had no idea we were there."

"Then why was Meredith at Miss New England Shooting Starz?" Delaney asked.

"To enter," Kylie replied. "She's one of the pageant contestants."

Lexi gulped. "Oh, I feel queasy."

"Maybe it's not so bad." Sadie tried to be optimistic. "I mean, so what if Meredith is in the pageant? We just drop off our cupcake delivery and go."

"Or we don't," Jenna said, raising an eyebrow. "Maybe we teach that big-mouthed bully a lesson she'll never forget. Maybe we put her in her place once and for all."

Lexi suddenly perked up. "How?"

"Well, Meredith obviously thinks she's going to win Miss New England Shooting Starz," Jenna began.

"Obviously," Kylie replied. "She and her pageant coach were so full of themselves."

"So we beat her! How mad and embarrassed would Meredith be if someone else won the crown?"

"And how do we do that?" Lexi asked. "Meredith has a coach and everything."

"We enter someone who's better than her," Jenna insisted. "I've seen her dance. It shouldn't be too hard to find someone with more talent."

"I sing and dance," Delaney volunteered. "Do you people recall I was on the West End stage in *Pygmalion* just a few short months ago?"

"Only because you snuck on." Sadie chuckled. "I don't think that counts, Laney."

"Whatever! I'm still our best chance, right?"

Kylie put an arm around her friend. "You definitely are. I trip over my own two feet, and none of us can carry a tune."

"Hey! I'll have you know I sing every morning in my shower!" Jenna protested. She began to belt out the words to a Spanish pop song: "*Hoy quiero bailar solo contigo!*"

Delaney covered her ears. "Ouch! We said we wanted to beat Meredith—not deafen the audience!"

Mrs. Noonan poked her head out from the kitchen. "Girls, please keep it down! I just put Delaney's baby sister and brother down for a nap."

But it was too late. Tristan and Charlotte were already wailing.

"I got it, Mom," Delaney said, dragging Lexi with her. "We'll get them back to sleep."

She led Lexi upstairs to the nursery. "If you just sing them a lullaby, they settle down," Delaney explained. She began to softly croon Katy Perry's "Roar."

"That's a lullaby?" Lexi asked. "Whatever happened to 'Twinkle, Twinkle, Little Star' or 'Rock-a-bye Baby'?"

Delaney picked up Tristan in her arms. "They have better taste in tunes," she said. "Katy, Beyoncé, an occasional Ariana Grande…"

She pointed to Charlotte's crib. "You pick her up and try it."

Lexi lifted the baby out of the crib and gently rocked her back and forth. "So I sat quietly…agreed politely," she sang softly. Charlotte yawned. "You're gonna hear me roar…"

Delaney gasped. "Lex! You can sing!"

Lexi made a face. "Nah, not really. I just mostly hum to the radio."

"No, really!" Delaney insisted. "You have a gorgeous voice! You should be the one to compete against Meredith."

Lexi stared. "No way. I could never get up on a stage and sing in front of hundreds of people."

"Thousands, maybe even millions," Delaney pointed out. "The pageant is going to be on local Connecticut TV, remember?"

Lexi placed a sleepy Charlotte back in her crib. "That's even worse!" she whispered. "No way. I'm not doing it."

She returned to the living room and found the rest

of the cupcake club debating who was the worst singer among them.

"I think I am," Sadie said. "My mom says I'm totally tone deaf." She demonstrated a very off-key rendition of "Happy Birthday."

"I always mangle the lyrics," Jenna insisted. "I had to sing 'Santa Claus Is Coming to Town' in first grade chorus. You know the part about him making a list and checking it twice? I sang, 'He's making a list, chicken and rice!'"

Kylie cracked up. "We all stink!"

Delaney came bolting down the stars. "Not all of us!"

"Fine, we know you want to do it, Delaney," Jenna said.

"No, I don't! I think Lexi should enter the pageant."

A hush fell over the room. "Lexi? Lexi Poole?" Jenna said what everyone else was thinking. "Are we talking about the same girl?"

"I'm right here!" Lexi complained.

"She's an amazing singer," Delaney insisted, patting Lexi on the back. "I just heard her upstairs doing 'Roar,' and she sounds just like Katy Perry!"

"Do you want to do it?" Kylie asked Lexi.

"No!" Lexi crossed her arms and pouted. "I absolutely do not."

"But we'd coach you," Delaney continued. "And Jenna's mom could make you an amazing pageant gown."

"*Sí*," Jenna said. "My *mami* would definitely sew you something *precioso*."

Lexi stood up and stamped her foot on the floor. "Are you guys listening to me? I said no."

"Because you're afraid Meredith will beat you, right?" Kylie asked. "That she'll humiliate you and call you a loser."

Lexi nodded. "Exactly."

"And that's exactly the reason you should do it," Kylie continued. "To stand up to her and stop being afraid."

"Trust us," Delaney said, gently. "We'll be right behind you."

"Just think about it," Kylie added. "No monster was ever beaten without someone being brave enough to step up and challenge her."

Lexi knew that was true and that her friends were right. But did she have to challenge Meredith on a huge pageant stage in front of millions of strangers?

"Fine," she said, finally giving in. "I'll think about it. But no promises."

9

Pageants and Penguins

Lexi didn't have to think too long or hard about the pageant. The decision found her fourth period in study hall. Meredith skipped into the classroom with Abby trailing behind her. Ms. Rathbane wasn't there yet, and Lexi smelled trouble.

"Someone had spinach for lunch," Meredith said, giggling and pointing to Lexi's teeth. She tossed her bag down on the desk next to Lexi's. "Or are you just green with envy?"

Lexi felt her fists clenching. "Quit it, Meredith."

"Quit it? Quit what?" the bully replied. "Poor little Lexi the Loser. You don't like it when people pick on you? I don't like it when people ruin my makeup!"

"I said, quit it," Lexi repeated slowly and quietly.

"Or what?" Meredith asked.

Lexi summoned every ounce of courage she had: "Or I'll have to beat you in the Miss New England Shooting Starz Pageant."

Meredith's mouth fell wide open. "How do you know about that? And what do you mean you'll beat me?"

Lexi smiled sweetly, doing her best Meredith impression. "That's for me to know and you to find out."

She got up from her desk just as Ms. Rathbane was walking into the room.

"Excuse me, Ms. Rathbane. May I please go to the library and do some research?"

The teacher looked confused. "What kind of research, Lexi?"

Lexi glared at Meredith at the back of the room. "I need to look up some sheet music for a special project I'm working on."

"I don't see why not," Ms. Rathbane said, handing her a hall pass.

Lexi turned on her heel and skipped out of the room. She didn't even have to look back to know that there was steam coming out of Meredith's ears.

☆ ☮ ☆

"Nuh-uh! You didn't say that!" Kylie said, shaking her head in disbelief when Lexi found her after school in the teachers' lounge kitchen.

"I did! I told her I'd beat her. What was I thinking?"

"So you're entering the pageant?" Kylie asked.

Lexi nodded. "I guess. Do I have a choice? My parents said if I wanted to, they'd put in the paperwork and the entrance fee. They think it's a great way to boost my confidence and help me get more comfortable speaking in public."

Kylie knew getting up in front of a crowd was the last thing Lexi wanted to do. Lexi's big sister, Ava, was the outgoing one, not her—and she was always in Ava's shadow.

Jenna, Sadie, and Delaney all filed in for the PLC meeting. "What's on the agenda today, Kyles?" Jenna asked, pulling up a stool.

"No cupcakes." Kylie slammed her hand on the counter. "Today we're cooking up a Miss New England Shooting Starz contestant."

"You're doing it!" Delaney exclaimed, hugging Lexi. "Yay, Lexi!"

"Go, girl!" Sadie cheered.

"Why's everyone so happy in here?" Herbie teased, rushing in. He was always a few minutes late.

Kylie hushed them. "Oh, nothing. Just loving our latest order for a penguin-themed fifth b-day party."

Herbie didn't look very convinced. "You guys are jumping up and down about penguins?"

"They're cute. And waddly," Jenna insisted. "Can't a person love a penguin?"

"I suppose," Herbie said, scratching his head. "But I also get the impression there is something you girls aren't telling me."

"Who, us?" Kylie tried to cover. "Like Jenna said, we're psyched for penguins."

"Okay," Herbie replied. "I'm psyched to show you what I came up with to make your huge thousand-cupcake pageant order go quicker and more efficiently."

Kylie rolled her eyes. "Not another flour-nator."

"Better!" Herbie said. "I call this my 'pipe-o-matic.'" He produced a sketch of a long conveyor belt with piping bags hanging above it. "The cupcakes roll by, and the piping bag automatically squirts on the icing."

Lexi looked horrified. "Piping is an art form!" she shouted. "You can't just let some machine do it for you. Not if you want your cupcakes to look original and amazing."

Herbie stared at his sketch. "Art's great, but it's not efficient. How long would it take you to pipe a hundred cupcakes?"

Lexi did some quick calculations on her fingers. "Maybe a half hour? I can probably do a cupcake every ten to fifteen seconds, depending on how complicated the design is."

"I estimate that my machine can do a hundred cupcakes in ten minutes flat," Herbie insisted. "That's saving you twenty minutes. And time is money."

"He has a point," Sadie said. "With an extra twenty minutes, we could do more cupcakes or even get a second order in the oven."

"We can't sacrifice quality for quantity," Kylie said, backing up Lexi. "I think this pipe-o-matic thing is a bad idea."

"Suit yourselves," Herbie said, rolling the plans up and tucking them in his bag. "If you're not willing to grow your business…"

"We are willing," Kylie insisted. "But not with machines that take the place of people. The best part of being in PLC is working together."

Jenna elbowed her. "I dunno. Maybe we need to see it in action. Do you think you could build a mini version and show us how it works?"

"Sure," Herbie answered. "I could probably put something rough together and have it ready for you next week."

"No! We need it now. I think you should go home and

get right on it," Jenna said, handing him his jacket. "The sooner, the better."

"At least someone here is enthusiastic about my ideas," Herbie said.

"*Buena suerte!* Good luck!" Jenna said, pushing him out the door. "Can't wait to see your pipe-o-macallit."

"Pipe-o-matic," Herbie corrected her as they closed the door behind him and locked it.

"I thought he would never leave!" Kylie said. "Good work, Jenna. We need to start coaching Lexi."

"Do you know how to walk?" Delaney asked her.

"Do I know how to walk?" Lexi replied, puzzled. "Don't I walk every day?"

"No," Delaney said, standing up and striking a pose. "I mean runway walk."

She strutted across the floor, gazed backward over her shoulder, shook her hips, and crisscrossed the floor in a T pattern.

"And what makes you an expert?" Sadie asked.

"Are you kidding?" Delaney answered. "I've watched a gazillion Miss America pageants and *Kim of Queens* episodes on TV. I know *exactly* how these things work."

She dragged Lexi to her feet. "Start at the far left corner.

Head up. Shoulders back. Hands at your sides. Now come toward me. And don't forget to sparkle!"

Lexi obeyed, but her walk looked more like a sprint.

"Slowly! Slowly!" Delaney barked. "Let the judges get a good look."

Lexi's face went white. "Get a good look? At me?"

"No, at the frosting on a cupcake! Of course, at you!"

Lexi sighed. "I don't know about this, guys. I feel really awkward—and I'm afraid I might pass out onstage in front of the judges."

"Not to mention the hundreds of people in the audience and the millions watching on TV," Jenna reminded her again.

"I can't! I can't!" Lexi started to back away. "This is a terrible idea."

Kylie grabbed her by the shoulders. "Keep your eyes on the prize."

"The crown? Who cares about a stupid crown?" Lexi exclaimed.

"No! Beating Meredith. Making her see that she can't put you down."

Lexi mulled it over. "Okay, I'll try."

"It'll look better in high heels," Delaney assured her.

"High heels? I can't walk in high heels!" Lexi shrieked.

Delaney put her arm around her friend. "You can, and you will. Miss Delaney is going to coach you."

"And Miss Jenna is going to have her *madre* sew your gown. Think of me as your style coach."

"I'll coach interview," Kylie said. "We'll write you an amazing intro and practice the Q and A so you'll be prepared for anything the judges ask you."

"And I'll handle the fitness category," Sadie volunteered. "When I'm done with you, you'll be able to dribble a basketball behind your back."

"You guys are great," Lexi said. "I just hope I don't disappoint you and make a fool of myself."

"You have nothing to worry about," Kylie said reassuringly. "It's Meredith who should be nervous."

Here Comes the Sun

Lexi had only worn a pair of high heels once—to her cousin's wedding. But Delaney was determined that she learn to master a three-inch heel. Delaney placed a math textbook on Lexi's head to remind her of her posture.

"Gracefully," she instructed her friend. "Not like you're walking on thin ice." Lexi practiced walking around the hardwood floor of her living room, trying her best not to teeter or fall. The book slammed onto the floor.

"They make my ankles all wobbly," Lexi complained. "And this big, poufy skirt keeps catching on them."

Jenna's mother, Betty, adjusted the long layers at the back of Lexi's gown. "*No problema,*" she said. "I'll fix it." Jenna's mom, Betty, had outdone herself, taking an old, lavender satin prom dress from Jenna's sister Gabby and beading the strapless bodice with white pearls and clear sequins so it glittered. The skirt was shimmery, purple tulle.

"You look like *una princesa*," Betty said, pinning up the hem ever so slightly.

Delaney took out her clipboard and checked off "Gown." She scanned the list. "I'm only giving you half a check for walking," she told Lexi. "You've got some work to do in that department."

"Whoa, you're a tough coach." Sadie chuckled. "Let me know when you want to practice her dribble." They had decided they would train all weekend for the pageant. With only three weeks left till the big day, time was flying by.

"Fitness after we work on talent," Delaney insisted. "We still don't have a song lined up."

Lexi twirled a strand of hair around her finger. "About that…"

"Broadway show tunes always score well, but if you really want to impress, I'd suggest an opera aria," Delaney said thoughtfully. She cleared her throat. "You know, 'Me, me, me, me'!"

"It's not me, me, me, me," Lexi said, sighing. "I've never sung in public before, Laney. I don't think I can do it."

"Of course you have! You sang in front of my baby

sister and brother—and they loved it. They gave you a napping ovation."

"Remember how I got horrible stage fright when we did *Romeo and Juliet* at school? And that was just speaking lines. Now you want me to sing them?"

"What if we get Jeremy here?" Jenna teased her. "You can serenade him with a love song."

"I'm not sure that's such a good idea," Lexi replied. "We're barely speaking. He's still mad at me over the blowup in the hallway."

"I think you should find a song you can connect to," Delaney said. She pored over a book of show tunes. "'Everything's Coming Up Roses'? 'Don't Rain on My Parade'? 'I Whistle a Happy Tune'?"

"I can't whistle either," Lexi said, pouting. "This is hopeless."

"Wait! What about this one!" Delaney said, shoving the sheet music under her nose.

"'Shy'?" Lexi gasped.

"It's a song from *Once Upon a Mattress*. It's the story of the princess and the pea."

"Lexi knows she's shy," Jenna piped up. "I don't think we need to advertise it."

"There must be *something* that you'd feel comfortable singing, Lexi," Kylie continued. "Some song that you love and know by heart."

Jenna nodded. "*Sí*, like '*Duérmete, Mi Niña*, right, Mami?"

Her mom laughed. "I don't think Lexi wants to sing that! It's telling a baby to sleep so the mom can wash the diapers and do the sewing! That was my lullaby for you and your brothers and sisters."

"My mom used to sing me a song when I was little and couldn't fall asleep," Lexi recalled. "But could I really sing 'You Are My Sunshine' at the pageant?"

"Why not?" Kylie said. "And you could wear a golden yellow dress when you sing it—something sunny."

Jenna's mom nodded. "*Sí*, I could make you a dress that looks like *el sol*."

"Then it's settled," Delaney said, placing a check next to "Talent" on her list. "You're pageant perfect, Lex!"

Kitchen Catastrophe

Herbie insisted that PLC hear him out before they put the finishing touches on the pageant order.

"I know you're set in your ways," he said, "but sometimes it's good to shake things up a bit."

He rolled a strange-looking machine into the teachers' lounge where they were working. It looked a lot like a treadmill with a pillowcase hanging from a shower curtain above it.

"What is that thing?" Kylie asked.

"None other than my pipe-o-matic," Herbie replied proudly. "I tested it out in the robotics lab, and I think it will work like a charm."

Lexi looked at the ingredients piled high on the counter. They'd managed to get fifty dozen cupcakes done the past two nights at Kylie's house, working till nearly midnight. Another thirty-three dozen still needed to be baked and decorated.

"We can do half today, half tomorrow," Jenna suggested.

"It's still a lot to do and a lot to assemble," Lexi pointed out. She stared at the calendar on the wall—the pageant was Saturday morning, and it was already Thursday afternoon.

"Precisely my point," Herbie said. "Give the pipe-o-matic a go."

Kylie hesitated, then saw Lexi's frantic expression. "Lex, you probably should be home with Delaney running your pageant routines, not worrying about the last batch of cupcakes," she said.

"But how will you ever get this all done?" Lexi said, sighing. "I can't just abandon you."

"You're not abandoning us," Sadie insisted. "You already made all the gold fondant stars and the pulled-sugar tiara for the top of the tower. We can handle the rest."

"I promise! My machine will be a huge help," Herbie assured them.

Jenna handed Lexi her backpack and gave her a push toward the door. "*Ir a casa*. Go home!" she said.

When Delaney and Lexi had left, Herbie began tinkering with his pipe-o-matic. "Can we get the frosting ready?" he asked, opening the large sack suspended from the rod.

"Yeah," Kylie said, tasting the white chocolate butter-cream on her fingertip. "We have one batch done. How much can that thing hold?"

"Let's see," Herbie calculated. "If that mixing bowl holds five quarts, I'd say my pipe-o-matic piping bag can hold about twenty-five quarts."

"Whoa!" Sadie gasped. "That's a lot of frosting."

"Which means you don't have to keep refilling the bag," Herbie explained. He'd attached a large metal cone to the bottom of the sack. "The machine uses air pressure to squeeze the bag. A few puffs and the cupcake is all piped. Then the conveyor belt moves it on its merry way."

"Hmm," Kylie said, examining the machine. "And how fast do the cupcakes move across the belt?"

"One every few seconds, but I can crank it up even faster if you want," Herbie bragged.

Jenna handed him a platter of cooled cupcakes. "Here's two dozen. I say we give Herbie's thingamabob a whirl."

"Pipe-o-matic," he corrected her. He checked all the settings as the girls whipped up five more bowls of frosting. When he was done scraping them into the sack, he stepped back, cracked his knuckles, and took a deep breath.

"Here goes nothing!" he said.

Kylie covered her eyes. "I can't watch. Tell me when it's over!"

At first, the machine sputtered and sparked. But eventually, the conveyor belt started up and a cupcake moved in under the pipe-o-matic nozzle.

"It's working!" Herbie cheered. With a loud *plop*, a dollop of frosting landed right on the cupcake. Sadie picked it up.

"Okay, that's pretty cool," she said. "I mean, it's not anywhere near as artistically beautiful as if we piped it. But it's not bad. Not bad at all."

She held the cupcake up for Kylie to examine. She opened one eye.

"I guess it's okay," she said.

"Okay? It's brilliant!" Herbie patted himself on the back. "A machine that frosts cupcakes at the speed of light."

"Um, I don't want to sound like Debbie Downer here," Jenna interrupted. "But that was pretty slow. So far, I'm not impressed."

"Stand back!" Herbie said, "I'm cranking her up to full power."

Again, the machine made some funny noises—a few pops, burps, and gurgles—then started up. *Plop!* One cupcake was frosted. *Plop!* Then another. *Plop!* Then another.

"Can it go faster?" Jenna asked. *Plop! Plop! Plop!* The cupcakes whizzed down the belt as Kylie caught them on the other side and placed them on platters.

"Check it out!" Herbie called over the humming motor. "I call this mode 'warp speed.'" Suddenly, the cupcakes were flying across the machine, faster than the girls could grab them off.

"Wait!" Kylie called. "Slow it down a bit!"

Herbie pushed several buttons but nothing happened. The belt had now run out of cupcakes and was still squirting frosting everywhere.

"No worries!" Herbie replied. "I installed an emergency brake." He pulled on a lever and it came off in his hand. "Whoopsie!"

Now, the sack was swelling up with air. Sadie tugged on Herbie's sweater sleeve. "Uh-oh!" She pointed above their heads. "That doesn't look good."

"No worries! No worries!" Herbie continued reassuring them as he frantically tried to make the machine stop piping. "If I can just figure out where I plugged it in…"

"I once overfilled my basketball with an air pump," Sadie told Kylie and Jenna.

"What happened?" Jenna asked.

"You don't want to know," Sadie replied. "But I think we should duck for cover."

She grabbed the girls, and they hid behind the kitchen counter.

Suddenly, there was a loud *Bang!* and white frosting exploded all over the teachers' lounge, ceiling to floor and wall to wall.

"*Dios mío!*" Jenna cried, surveying the damage.

"You can say that again," Kylie exclaimed. Then she noticed Herbie standing in the center of the room, his entire head buried under a mountain of white chocolate buttercream. He looked like the Abominable Snowman.

"Herbie? You okay?" she called.

He wiped his glasses—which were covered in frosting—with the back of his hand.

"Yeah. I'm fine. But I feel like a giant cupcake." He licked his lips. "Tastes good though."

The girls slipped and slid their way over to him, stepping in the sticky icing. "Principal Fontina is gonna kill us," Sadie said.

"Look on the bright side," Kylie said, trying to cheer up Herbie. "You can use your flour-nator to clean it all up in a jiffy."

Herbie frowned. "I don't think the flour-nator can make a dent in this mess," he said. "I think we'll have to do it. After I go change into something a little less frosted."

He stumbled out of the room.

"So much for making our pageant order go faster," Jenna said, sighing. "Now we have all this to clean up on top of it. We'll be here all night."

Mr. Mullivan and a few of his custodians peered into the room. "I heard the explosion," he said. "I don't want to know what happened, but I assume Mr. Dubois had something to do with it."

Kylie nodded. "He meant well. But now we're in a real bind. Can you help us, Mr. Mullivan?"

"Tell you what, girls," the custodian said, resting his mop against the wall. "My staff and I will clean this mess up in no time—if you bake us a dozen of your best cupcakes." He wiped a smudge of frosting off the wall and took a taste. "I have a serious sweet tooth."

"Deal!" Kylie said.

"And if you need some help, I'm pretty good in the kitchen myself. And a few of the guys aren't bad bakers either. Mr. Gordon here makes a mean fruitcake at Christmas."

Kylie looked at the clock on the wall. They had already wasted forty-five minutes.

"Gentlemen," she asked, smiling. "Who needs an apron?"

Pageant Day

Thanks to the custodial staff's quick cleanup—and help baking—the order was all ready by Saturday morning. Lexi, however, wasn't ready. She'd tossed and turned all night. She had a horrible dream that when she got onstage to sing at the pageant, everyone in the audience booed and hissed. "Wait! Stop! Give me a chance!" she cried in her nightmare. Her mom shook her awake.

"Honey, you're dreaming," she said. "Wake up."

Lexi sat up in bed. She felt cold and clammy and out of breath. "It was the worst nightmare I've ever had!" she exclaimed.

"Really? Worse than the one about all your paintbrushes getting sucked up into a flying saucer and taken to outer space?" her mom asked.

"Okay, that one was *really* bad too," Lexi admitted.

"But this was worse. I was the laughingstock of the Miss New England Shooting Starz Pageant!"

"It was just a dream," her mom said, planting a kiss on Lexi's forehead. "And you know what dreams are, right?"

Lexi sighed. She knew her mom was about to launch into one of her long-winded medical explanations. This is what she got for having a mother who was a veterinarian!

"A dream is just images, sounds, and sensations we experience when we sleep," her mom said. "Often, they're just our fears and anxieties fighting to be heard."

"I know that," Lexi said. "And I know I'm super nervous about making a fool of myself tomorrow—which is why I'm dreaming about it."

"You mean today," her mom said, glancing at the clock. "It's 6:00 a.m."

"What?" Lexi yelped, jumping out of bed. "I have to curl my hair! And polish my nails! And practice my speech! Delaney will be here by seven, and I'm not even up yet!"

She ran past her mom into the bathroom and began setting her hair in hot rollers. When Delaney arrived, Lexi was swiping on mascara and lip gloss and walking around her room in her pj's and pageant heels.

"Is that your evening-gown look?" Delaney teased.

"These peace sign pj's are cute, but I think I liked the rainbow unicorns more."

"You told me to practice walking in my heels—so I'm walking in my heels," Lexi huffed. "And I've recited my speech about a hundred times."

"Relax," Delaney said, flopping down on her friend's bed. "You are more than ready."

"I don't feel more than ready," Lexi said, staring in the mirror. "I feel like a disaster."

"You're going to do great," her big sister Ava said. She was standing in the doorway. "I brought you something." She handed Lexi a small velvet box. When she opened it, there was a tiny silver horseshoe necklace inside. "For luck. It helped me win all my spelling bees, debates, class president election…"

"You win everything." Lexi sighed.

Ava took the necklace out of the box and fastened it around Lexi's neck. "And now you will too."

☆ ☮ ☆

Lexi's mom, dad, and sister drove with her and Delaney to the hotel where the pageant was taking place. "We'll park and meet you inside," her mom said, planting a kiss on Lexi's cheek. "You'll do great, honey."

"Break a leg, squirt," her father added.

"Actually, don't break a leg—that would be embarrassing," her sister chimed in. "Just win a big prize, like a giant plasma TV."

"So you can put it in your bedroom?" Lexi teased.

"Exactly!" Ava replied. "But I'll be a really nice sister and let you watch it when I'm not home."

The girls unloaded the bags from the trunk and went to check in and get the lay of the land. A large crowd was already assembling in the grand ballroom, and girls were pouring into the hotel lobby with their moms, coaches, and enough sparkling evening gowns to stock an entire department store.

"Excuse me," said a tiny blond carrying a large duffel bag. Lexi noticed she had a Southern twang to her voice. "Do y'all know where we drop off our things for talent?"

Lexi shook her head. "No, I'm sorry. I'm new to this whole pageant thing and totally lost."

The girl smiled. "Well, why don't you come with me? We'll figure it out together." She seemed so smart and confident and super friendly. Maybe not everyone was like Meredith, bent on winning no matter what.

"Have you done this before? Pageants, I mean?" Lexi asked as they followed the signs pointing to the dressing rooms.

"Oh yes! I'm Miss Preteen Atlanta Dreams," the girl said sweetly. "It's no biggie."

"You won?" Lexi gasped. "You won a whole pageant?"

"A bunch, actually," the girl replied. "I love competing—it's kinda my thing. Along with silks." She pulled two long strips of fabric out of her duffel bag.

"What do you do with those?" Lexi asked. She'd never seen anything like them.

"Well, we hang 'em from the ceiling, and I do this kind of upside-down aerial dance."

"Wow," Lexi exclaimed. "That is so cool. Way cooler than what I do."

"What do you do?" the girl asked.

"I sing. Just sing."

"Well, I think that's amazing," the pageant pro replied. "I can't sing worth a lick. My mom says I sound like a cat getting her tail pulled."

Lexi giggled. "I'm Lexi Poole."

"And I'm Harleigh Park." She smiled brightly. "Poole and Park. We could be a great song-and-dance act. If you promise to do all the singing!"

Just then, the girls noticed a commotion coming from outside the hotel entrance.

"Move it!" shouted a woman dressed in a red suit and large sunglasses. She was bossing around a bellboy as he struggled to unload stuff from her car onto a luggage rack. There were dozens of garment bags, shoe boxes, and something that vaguely resembled a giant silver crescent moon.

"Who does she think she is?" Harleigh asked. "They haven't crowned a queen yet."

Lexi didn't even have to look to know who was trailing behind the woman in red. "She's kind of the queen bee at my school," she explained. "Her name is Meredith Mitchell."

"You know her?" Harleigh asked. "Are you friends?"

"Oh no!" Lexi laughed. "She hates my guts."

Meredith was also wearing a pair of large sunglasses, but that didn't stop Lexi from sensing her cold stare. "She was mean to me, and I kinda said I was going to beat her today," Lexi added. "Stupid, huh?"

"Nuh-uh!" Harleigh insisted. "I'm rooting for you. Besides, good always conquers evil."

Lexi grinned. "Funny, that's what my friend Kylie always says. But she's usually talking about monster movies."

"Well, she's right," Harleigh said. Her very blond mom

was waving at her from across the floor. "I gotta go. But I'll catch up with you later. K?"

"K," Lexi answered. It was probably a good idea to find out where Delaney had wandered off to. Lexi found her friend chatting up the pageant host, a jovial man in a tuxedo named Mr. Jim.

"So, here's the scoop," Delaney whispered to Lexi when they were out of the host's earshot. "You need to win as many of the categories as possible if you want to qualify for one of the supreme titles."

"Meaning?" Lexi asked.

"Meaning you have to place top in interview, talent, and fitness," Delaney explained.

"I might as well go home now," Lexi fretted. There was no way she was going to win all of those categories—much less even one of them!

"You can do it. I believe in you," Delaney said.

"We do too!" Kylie suddenly appeared behind her. The other girls had dropped off the cupcakes in the ballroom and were waiting for Sadie's dad to assemble the display he'd built.

"We brought a whole cheering section, *chica*," Jenna said. She pointed to Kylie's mom, Jenna's mom, and Herbie, who were all purchasing wristbands to attend the pageant.

"Save me a seat," Delaney reminded them. "We've gotta go get ready for gowns." She pulled poor Lexi along with her. "Remember everything I told you: shoulders back, head up, walk slowly…"

It was so much to think about! Lexi's head was spinning as Delaney led her to the dressing room and helped her into her long gown. There was lots of noise, along with endless racks of clothes, and dozens of girls were getting primped and prepped for the pageant.

"What if I forget which way to go?" Lexi asked her friend. "What if I suddenly go left when I'm supposed to go right?"

Delaney zipped up the back of Lexi's dress. "You'll be fine. Smile and sparkle."

A voice suddenly boomed over the loudspeaker. "Ladies, this is Fitzy. Please line up backstage according to your contestant number. Ten minutes till pageant time!"

Lexi felt her heart leap out of her chest. "Oh my gosh! Ten minutes!"

Harleigh found her and gave her hand a squeeze. "You look beautiful," she said. "Purple is definitely your color." Lexi saw that Harleigh was wearing a white gown with a sweetheart neckline and intricate rhinestone beading on the bodice.

"You look beautiful too," Lexi said.

"And look, I'm number sixteen and you're number fifteen. So we get to stand next to each other!"

Having Harleigh at her side made Lexi feel a tiny bit better, but then she spied Meredith making her way down the hall in a billowing, red-sequin ball gown.

"She looks like that evil queen from *Alice in Wonderland*," Delaney whispered. "You know—the one who shouts, 'Off with her head!'"

Lexi reached for her neck. "Not helping, Laney," she said, secretly wishing there was a rabbit hole she could duck down.

"You'll be fine," Harleigh assured her. "If you need help, I'll be right there beside you."

Then Lexi saw something that made her stomach do a sickening flip-flop. Meredith was wearing a ribbon that read "14," which meant Lexi would be standing right next to her as well!

"Go, go!" Delaney said, smoothing Lexi's skirt and pushing her toward the ballroom. "Five minutes."

When they got backstage, Lexi tried not to bump into Meredith. She hoped she wouldn't notice that they were standing next to each other, but no such luck. Miss Jen pushed Meredith into the line. Meredith's face fell.

"*You!*" she screamed. "Why are *you* next to me?"

Lexi shrugged. "Lucky, I guess."

"Don't talk to her," Miss Jen instructed Meredith. "Focus! Be fierce. When you get up there on the runway, look the judges dead in the eye and own this pageant."

Thankfully, Meredith turned her back on Lexi so she could get "in the zone," as her coach called it. Lexi breathed a sigh of relief. A cold shoulder she could handle; it was better than a fistfight.

Hershey was racing around backstage, checking names and numbers on a clipboard, and making sure everyone was in place and ready to go. She stopped to straighten Lexi's ribbon.

"Good luck!" she said, smiling.

Lexi took several deep breaths, trying to calm the feeling of terror rising in her chest. What was she thinking? How could she possibly enter a pageant, much less beat Meredith Mitchell?

But it was too late to run—Laura and Fitzy were onstage welcoming the audience, and Mr. Jim was already announcing the contestants. As each girl walked out, she took the microphone and introduced herself. Each had a catchy two-minute speech outlining who they were, where they were from, what they loved to do, and what they wanted to be. There were lots of future doctors, fashion designers, Broadway stars, Presidents of the United States—even a pig farmer. But Meredith's intro was definitely the most memorable!

"Meredith Mitchell, that's my name!" she rapped, right there in her long gown.

"I don't want money; I don't want fame!"

"She doesn't?" Kylie asked. She was seated in the audience with the rest of the PLC entourage. "Are we talking about the same Meredith Mitchell?"

"Gonna make the world better—one step at a time

And tell you 'bout myself in rhythm and rhyme.

Be kind to people, generous and true.

A message of compassion from me to you!"

The judges beamed and the audience applauded wildly.

"How am I supposed to follow that?" Lexi asked Harleigh.

"Just speak from the heart," she replied. "Anyone can see that girl is as phony as a three-dollar bill!"

Lexi took a deep breath, touched the lucky horseshoe pendant around her neck, and stepped out onto the stage. *Here goes nothing!*

Mr. Jim handed her the mic.

"Hello," she said softly into it.

"Speak up!" Mr. Jim reminded her.

"Hello!" she tried again. "My name is Lexi Poole, and I'm twelve years old and a proud member of Peace, Love, and Cupcakes, the best cupcake-baking business in Connecticut."

"Hey! I've had those cupcakes and they're awesome!" shouted a boy's voice from the back of the audience.

Lexi blushed. "I used to be really shy, and I've learned that everyone needs to find her voice. Everyone has something to say and deserves to be heard. So that's why I'm here today. To prove that no one can hold you down if you speak up for yourself." She glanced at Meredith in the wings before adding "thank you" and strutting down the runway confidently. She tried to remember everything Delaney had told her—especially the part about looking the judges in the eye and "sparkling." When she reached the far right corner of the stage, Mr. Jim nodded at her and she stepped off.

"Thank you, Lexi," he said. The judges applauded and jotted down notes.

"You did it, girl!" Harleigh cheered as Lexi made her way backstage again.

"Your turn," Lexi said, hugging her. "Go get 'em!"

"Hi, y'all," Harleigh said brightly. "I am the

gymnastics queen! With my flips and twists, I love to soar. My dream is to win a gold medal at the Olympics and make my parents and my country proud. I have faith that I can change the world, and I will do my best to help those in need. My guilty pleasure is making homemade pumpkin pie with my granny—it's the best! From Atlanta, Georgia, I am Harleigh Park."

"That was so good!" Lexi congratulated her after her runway walk. "You're so relaxed and real. I wish I could be more like you."

"You were perfect," Harleigh told her.

"Perfectly awful," said an icy voice behind them.

Lexi steeled her nerves and ignored Meredith's snarky comment.

"That's right," Harleigh whispered. "Don't you listen to anything she says. You're way better than her."

"Oh, we'll see who's better," Meredith smirked. "My talent routine is up next."

13

Unlucky Star

"Now *that's* a costume," Ava remarked as Meredith stepped onstage. She was dressed in a black-velvet catsuit covered in gold stars. The lights dimmed, and the stars lit up and flashed to the beat of the music.

"You must be my lucky star!" Meredith sang the Madonna hit as she tap-danced across the stage while simultaneously twirling a pair of batons in the air.

"A totally electrified costume," Herbie marveled. Jenna shot him a nasty look.

"I'm not saying she should win or anything—just that from a technological standpoint, it's nifty," he added.

"Her singing and dancing isn't nifty," Delaney groaned, holding her ears. "It's awful. Lexi is way better than her."

But the judges didn't seem to mind. They were mes-merized by Meredith's impressive backdrop—a black sky that flashed the words "STAR" in neon lights. In the center of the stage was a giant silver crescent moon.

"What do you suppose that thing does?" Sadie asked. It was a split second before she had the answer. The moon suddenly floated up in the air as Meredith performed below it.

"Amazing," Herbie gushed. "Hydraulics as well."

"It's all flash and no substance," Kylie insisted. "Typical Meredith." But she watched the judges' faces and saw how easily impressed they were. As much as she hated to admit it, Meredith was stiff competition.

At the end of the song, Meredith bowed and tossed her baton high in the air. It flew up, up, up, right over the moon, but as it came down, it just missed her grasp. The audience watched in horror as it landed with a *thud* right on one of the judge's heads.

"Oh! My head! My head!" the judge cried.

"Do we have a doctor in the house?" Mr. Jim announced in a panic over the microphone. "Our judge, Kat Grabel, needs a doctor!"

Lexi's mom raced from her seat. "I'm a doctor," she said, examining the judge, a former Miss Georgia. There was a huge goose egg on her forehead.

"How many fingers am I holding up?" Dr. Poole asked her.

Kat squinted. "Two? Maybe four? I don't know, y'all!"

"Let's get some ice on that bump," Dr. Poole said. "I think you'll be okay."

Kat looked at Meredith's backdrop. "But I'm seeing stars!" she moaned.

"That's the set—not your eyes," Dr. Poole assured her.

Meredith looked terrified—not that she had hurt Kat, but that she'd hurt her chances of winning the pageant. "It just slipped out of my hand," she pleaded. "It's not my fault."

Kat glared at her. "And it's not my fault if I deduct ten points from your score for assaulting a judge!"

Meredith tried to sweet-talk her. "Miss Grabel, I am your biggest fan. I watched your winning aria as Miss Georgia on YouTube a gazillion times."

That seemed to calm the furious judge down. "You don't say?"

"I would *never* purposely hit you on the head with a baton," Meredith continued, crossing her fingers over her still-glowing costume. "Cross my heart."

When she returned backstage, Miss Jen quickly pulled

her to a side. "Nice save," she said. "You played that judge like a violin."

"Of course I did," Meredith said. "There's no way she's going to deduct any points. In fact, I bet she gives me a perfect score for that perfect suck-up speech I just made."

Harleigh's silks routine was next, and it was flawless. She whirled and twirled in the air to the song "Amazing Grace," wrapping the silks delicately around her arms and legs.

"You did great!" Lexi applauded her.

"It was okay, not my best." Harleigh shrugged. "I kinda slipped up at the end."

"I didn't notice," Lexi assured her. "And at least you didn't give any of the judges a concussion like *some* people." She knew Meredith was standing right there and heard her.

"Up next," Mr. Jim called, "please welcome to the stage contestant number fifteen, Lexi."

"Oh my gosh! That's me!" Lexi panicked.

"Deep breaths!" Harleigh tried to calm her. "And here's a little trick: Don't look at the entire audience. Just find one face and focus on it—one of the judges is a good idea. That's what I do."

Lexi crept out onstage and cleared her throat.

"She looks terrified," Delaney whispered to Kylie. "Shake it off, Lex! Shake it off!"

"I hope she doesn't faint…again," Jenna said, crossing her fingers. "We don't need a repeat of *Romeo and Juliet* on local Connecticut TV."

Lexi felt queasy. There were so many people, and they were all staring at her! She tried to focus on Kat Grabel's spiky platinum-blond hair, but the room started to spin. She couldn't catch her breath or steady herself. Just then, she saw a hand shoot up from the back row. "Lexi! Over here!" shouted a voice. The person stood up on his seat and waved.

Lexi's eyes met his—it was Jeremy! He had come to cheer her on. He was there for her, not for Meredith. He was still her boyfriend and he cared! She focused on his face as the music began to play.

"You make me happy when skies are gray," Lexi sang sweetly, right to Jeremy. Everything else blurred away. All she could see was him. "You'll never know, dear, how much I love you…"

When she was done, she looked at the judges. Kat Grabel was sobbing, and she was pretty sure it was not because her head hurt. In fact, a lot of people in the audience were teary—especially Lexi's mom, who had taught her that song so many years ago.

"Oh, Lexi," Harleigh said, hugging her as she came off stage. "That was absolutely beautiful."

Lexi shrugged. "You think so? I kind of zoned out and did what you said. I just focused on Jeremy. Do you think the judges liked it?"

"You sang from your heart," Harleigh replied. "How could they not?"

14

And the Winner Is...

Lexi barely had a chance to catch her breath. There were still two more categories left to complete: fitness and interview. She ducked back into the dressing room and came out wearing a Blakely Bears basketball uniform that Sadie had lent her. Meredith spotted her and started laughing.

"Are you kidding me? You call *that* a fitness outfit?" She was dressed in a flashy Zumba costume.

"Come on, Lexi," Harleigh said, stepping between them. She was wearing a royal-blue ice-skating costume with a pair of white figure skates tossed over her shoulder.

"Thanks for rescuing me," Lexi whispered as they made their way backstage.

"What are friends for?" Harleigh smiled. "That Meredith certainly has a bee in her bonnet."

Lexi watched as Meredith exploded onto the stage chanting, "Shake it! Shake it!"

In the audience, Jenna winced. "She looks like she's got *hormigas en sus pantalones*—ants in her pants!"

Kat Grabel looked confused as Meredith spun wildly across the stage.

"I think the judges agree with you," Delaney told Jenna.

"Kat's probably scared she's gonna get conked on the noggin again," Lexi's dad piped up. "That girl is a health hazard."

Meredith ended her routine without incident—and blew kisses to the crowd.

"Top that!" she dared Lexi as she pushed past her. "I know you won't, Lexi the Loser."

Lexi gulped, then heard Mr. Jim announce her number. She walked out onstage, basketball in hand, and stood there, frozen.

"Dribble it! Dribble it!" Sadie willed her telepathically from the audience.

Lexi's music, Pharrell's "Happy," was playing, but she didn't seem to hear it, nor did she look too happy. Finally, as she reached the end of the runway, she bounced the ball once.

"She forgot everything I taught her!" Sadie groaned.

"It's that evil Meredith," Delaney said. "She must have said something to freak her out."

"Pass it here!" Sadie suddenly shouted. She stood up on her seat and held her hands up for Lexi to throw her the ball.

Lexi looked like she was in a trance.

"Come on, Lex," Sadie yelled. "Shoot the ball! You can do it!"

Lexi took a deep breath and tossed the ball high in the air, aiming for Sadie's voice. Sadie reached up and caught it effortlessly.

"Now that's what I call a slam dunk," Kat Grabel whispered to her fellow judges, who seemed equally impressed.

Lexi scrambled off the stage just as Harleigh was walking out into her routine. She pretended to whirl around the stage in her jazz shoes, shifting the skates from shoulder to shoulder and posing.

"I think we should go check on her before interviews," Delaney suggested. "She could probably use a little PLC pep talk."

"Allow me," Herbie said, getting out of his seat. "I believe I can help."

"That's what you said before you covered the entire teachers' lounge in frosting!" Kylie protested. "We're Lexi's friends. We know her best."

"But I was a shy kid with an older sister who

overshadowed me," Herbie insisted. Then he looked at Kylie. "Like you always tell me, 'I got this.'"

When he found Lexi backstage, she was pacing the floor.

"Feeling a bit wonky?" he asked her.

"Beyond wonky. I'm a wreck," she admitted. "I can't go out there and answer questions on the spot!"

"Because?" Herbie questioned.

"Because I don't know what they'll ask me. And I don't know what I'll say."

"You should simply say what comes to your mind—whatever it is," Herbie replied. He pulled up two chairs for them to sit down.

"Did I ever tell you about the Vancouver Robotics Competition?"

"Nope." Lexi shook her head. "But what does that have to do with me making a fool of myself at a pageant?"

"Well, it was a pageant of sorts—for robots though, not people," Herbie explained. "I built this brilliant robot named R23P-Ono who could hit golf balls."

Lexi sighed. "You've lost me, Herbie."

"Anyway, R2 should have won first place—clearly. Except that my big sister, Juliette, won an acting award the day before—a huge six-foot-tall gold trophy, no less."

"Again, I'm lost."

"Well, I thought, 'There's no way I can ever compete with her,'" Herbie continued. "'She's the winner in this family, not me.'"

Lexi started to understand. "So what happened to R2?"

"I overloaded his circuits. I doubted myself and tried to rethink all the programming right before the competition. I should have just believed in myself."

Lexi nodded. "You're saying I should just believe in myself. Not worry about Ava or Meredith or anyone else."

"Precisely," Herbie replied. "You shouldn't have to live up to anyone's expectations except your own."

Lexi stood up. "Okay. I'll try."

"Atta girl!" Herbie said, beaming. "And for the record, I think you are way more talented than my robot."

"Thanks—I think." Lexi smiled. She heard Meredith giving her response to a question—something about what she wanted most in the world.

"I want world peace!" Meredith said, clutching her hands to her heart. "I want an end to hunger. I want justice for all!"

In the audience, Jenna made a gagging noise. "I want to throw up. She is so phony."

Just then, she noticed Meredith's pageant coach in the row in front of them. Miss Jen was gesturing in the air, trying to tell Meredith something.

"What's with the charades?" she whispered to Delaney.

"Beats me," Delaney replied. "I don't speak sign language."

The coach continued waving her arms over her head and wrapping them around her shoulders.

"I want…I want…" Meredith tried to figure out what her coach's strange moves meant. "I want big hair? A hot-air balloon? A cashmere shawl?"

Miss Jen looked as nauseated as Jenna.

"Oh! I want to give a big hug to every kid who needs one! That's what I forgot!" Meredith finally got it.

The judges jotted notes as she skipped offstage. Miss Jen collapsed in her seat with a huge sigh of relief.

Lexi waited for Mr. Jim to call her number, then slowly made her way to the microphone. The host held an index card in his hand.

"Lexi, here is your question: What is your favorite thing to do in your spare time?"

Lexi gasped. That was it? That was the question? Nothing about politics, world peace, or global warming?

"We didn't practice that one," Kylie whispered to the girls. "I hope she's okay with it."

"That's easy," Lexi spoke confidently. "My favorite thing to do in my spare time is make cupcakes with my best friends in our cupcake club. We have an amazing business—in fact, we created an awesome display of one thousand cupcakes, and you can taste them at the pageant party…" She noticed Kat Grabel licking her lips. "I made the big pulled-sugar crown on top." The crowd oohed and ahhed.

"I'm really proud of how our club has grown, and how I've grown too," Lexi continued. "If it weren't for Peace, Love, and Cupcakes, I would never have figured out how to believe in myself." She looked at the audience and saw Herbie, who was giving her a thumbs-up.

"Thank you, Lexi," Mr. Jim said.

When it was Harleigh's turn, she cleared her throat and looked straight at the judges. "If you could be anyone in the world, who would you be?" Mr. Jim asked her. Harleigh thought for a minute, then replied. "I would be me," she said simply. "I don't think you should ever try to be someone you're not. You should always be true to yourself and celebrate what makes you unique and special." She glanced at Lexi in the wings and winked.

The judges applauded and Harleigh walked gracefully offstage. She found Lexi waiting for her. "You rocked it!" she said.

"I was going to say I wanted to be an Olympic gold medalist," Harleigh admitted. "Then I heard what you said, and it inspired me."

"Me? I inspired *you*?" Lexi asked. "But you're the one who's won so many pageants."

"And you're the one who has great friends who care about you and the coolest club I've ever heard of," Harleigh replied.

"And now I have another great friend," Lexi said, hugging her. "And you have an open invitation to come bake with us anytime."

☆ ☮ ☆

The judges deliberated for more than an hour. They handed out the awards for the youngest contestants first—the babies, toddlers, and five- to seven-year-olds. Lexi could barely stand still as Mr. Jim next went through the list of eight-, nine-, ten-, and eleven-year-old divisional titles.

Harleigh looked just as nervous. "I always think this is the hardest part of the whole pageant," she said. "The waiting."

Finally, it was time to announce the preteen queens. Lexi, Meredith, and Harleigh all took the stage with seven other girls as Mr. Jim held up a list from the judges. There were so many categories: Miss Congeniality, Miss Photogenic, Best Smile, Best Hair, Best Eyes. Lexi watched as one by one, girls went up to receive a trophy and a tiara. She, Harleigh, and Meredith were still standing there, crownless.

"For Best Costume, number fourteen, Meredith Mitchell," Mr. Jim read.

Meredith raced forward and snatched the trophy out of his hand.

"I'm not surprised," Harleigh whispered to Lexi. "Hers was very flashy—literally."

"Next, we have the award for Preteen Ultimate Talent," Mr. Jim read. Lexi squeezed Harleigh's hand. "You got this one," she whispered.

"The winner is number fifteen, Lexi Poole!" Lexi was stunned—there had to be some mistake! She had won for *singing*? It was crazy! She saw her parents, sister, friends, and Jeremy in the audience, jumping up and down and cheering.

Harleigh gave her a little push forward. "Go on!" she whispered. "I'm so proud of you!"

"Congratulations!" Fitzy said, pinning a huge, sparkling rhinestone crown on her head. As the cameras flashed, Lexi felt like she was having an out-of-body experience. Could this *really* be happening to her?

The rest of the crowning ceremony felt like a dream. Harleigh won Best Interview and Best Fitness, while Meredith took Best Gown.

"Do you think Lexi has a chance of winning the whole enchilada?" Jenna asked Delaney.

"Crazier things have happened," Delaney replied.

Jeremy moved up to the front row and sat there with his fingers and toes crossed.

Mr. Jim opened the envelope from the judges and prepared to the read the name on it—the Ultimate Grand Supreme for the entire pageant.

"Ladies and gentleman, please welcome your new Miss New England Shooting Starz, Harleigh Park!"

Harleigh opened her mouth to scream, but Meredith beat her to it.

"*Nooooo!*" she howled.

"Yes!" Lexi cried. "Harleigh, you did it! You won! You won!"

She watched as her friend received her banner and huge

crown from Fitzy and Laura. As Mr. Jim serenaded her, she walked the runway, waving to the crowd.

"It's not fair," Meredith complained. She tossed her tiara on the floor. "I should have won." Lexi was enjoying seeing Meredith utterly miserable, until she noticed the tears in Meredith's eyes.

"Hey," she said softly. "It's no big deal."

Meredith sniffled. "My coach and my parents are going to be furious."

"But you did your best," Lexi insisted. "And for what it's worth, Meredith, I thought you did a really great job."

Meredith's jaw dropped. "You did? You do?"

"Yeah, I mean the baton accident wasn't your finest moment, but you look really pretty."

Meredith looked down at her red ball gown. The skirt was now dotted with her tears.

"You too. I mean, you look better than you usually do. And your speech and talent were pretty good—for an amateur."

Lexi smiled. From Meredith, that was a major compliment!

Jeremy and the PLC girls raced to the edge of the stage to greet her.

"Give the woman some room," Delaney said, holding them back. "Make room for the Ultimate Talent Queen."

Lexi blushed. "Oh, it's no biggie."

"Are you kidding? My girlfriend is a pageant queen!" Jeremy said, planting a kiss on her cheek. Lexi loved the sound of the words "my girlfriend."

Ava was the next to grab her and pull her into a bear hug. "Lex, you were incredible! Who knew you had it in you?"

"I did," Herbie said. "But does anyone ever listen to me? Noooooo!"

"Maybe we should—once in a while," Lexi teased. "For an advisor, you do give pretty good advice."

"Then may I advise you now to go wheel in your cupcake tower before this crowd mutinies?" he said. "We have hungry people here who need Peace, Love, and One Thousand Cupcakes!"

☆ ☮ ☆

The PLC girls gathered in the reception room in front of their towering cupcake display.

"Dad, you deserve the crown for Best Builder," Sadie told her father.

"I love how the tower rotates," Kylie added,

admiring how the mirrored shelves gently spun and reflected the lights of the ballroom.

"Interesting," Herbie said, peering under the bottom shelf at the display's motor. "A simple but elegant mechanism."

Kat Grabel was the first judge to make her way into the after-party.

"Are these the cupcakes you mentioned in your speech?" she asked Lexi.

Lexi smiled. "Yes, try one, please!" She handed the judge a perfect pink velvet.

Kim took a nibble—then a huge bite. "Mmm, mmm! I wish I had a crown to give for Best Cupcake. Ladies, y'all would take the prize!"

Within minutes, all the contestants, judges, and audience members poured into the room and mobbed the cupcake display. Soon all that was left of the thousand cupcakes were a few crumbs.

"I'd say they liked them," Delaney said, elbowing Lexi. "That Kat lady especially. I think I saw her put a few in her purse!"

Laura reached up and took the sugar crown off the top of the display. "Would you mind if I kept this for my collection?" she asked Lexi.

"Sure, if you want it," Lexi replied, flattered.

Laura smiled. "And if you ever want to enter another Starz pageant, we would be proud to have you compete—with or without your amazing cupcakes."

Fitzy interrupted: "But preferably *with* cupcakes!" She had a white buttercream mustache over her top lip. "They're just *so* good."

15

Easy as Pumpkin Pie

By Sunday night, everything in Lexi's life was back to normal. She had gently placed her rhinestone crown on a shelf over her desk where she could admire it, and was working on her latest art homework—a painting of a rainbow unicorn—when her mom knocked on her bedroom door.

"There's someone here to see you," she said.

Lexi's face lit up when she got downstairs and recognized a familiar freckled face waiting in her living room.

"Harleigh!" she squealed. "What are you doing here?"

"My mom and I wanted to ask y'all a favor," she said. "My thirteenth birthday is coming up, and we were wondering if Peace, Love, and Cupcakes would bake for my party."

"All the way in Atlanta? I'm not sure how we'd get the cupcakes delivered to you," Lexi said.

"Well, you'd have to come to the party, of course," Harleigh's mom, Bobbie, replied.

"Really? Could we, Mom?" Lexi looked hopefully at her mother.

"Your dad and I do have some frequent-flyer miles saved up," she said. "I suppose we could fly down to Atlanta for a weekend."

"I know *exactly* what cupcakes to bake for you," Lexi said. "But I'm not telling. It's a surprise."

☆ ☮ ☆

When they boarded the plane to Atlanta six weeks later, the attendant helped Lexi place her cupcake carrier containing two dozen cupcakes in the overhead bin where it wouldn't bump around during the flight.

"Cupcakes, eh?" the man asked. "What kind are they?"

"Pumpkin pie cupcakes with cinnamon buttercream," Lexi answered. She reached into her backpack and pulled out a small box containing four extras. "Would you like to try one?"

The man's eyes lit up. "Would I? You just made my day! Is there anything better than pumpkin pie in the sky?"

She handed another one to her dad, who was seated next to her, and took one out for herself.

"It was nice of Harleigh's granny to give us her secret recipe," she said, taking a bite. The cinnamon and clove tickled her tongue. "Jenna was able to figure out a cupcake version in no time."

"I'm sure Harleigh will love them," her father remarked. "And the beautiful Olympic medals you made to go on top."

When they got to the party, Harleigh was happily racing around, greeting friends and family. She looked beautiful in a pink chiffon party dress and silver strappy sandals.

"Lexi!" she said, running over to her as Lexi and her dad walked through the white picket gate out front. "I'm so glad you came! Wait till you see all the decorations—we did a whole Barbie theme—and the karaoke setup!"

"Karaoke?" Lexi asked. "As in you sing into a microphone? In front of everybody?" Lexi could feel her heart start to pound.

"Yup!" Harleigh said. Then she remembered that Lexi didn't love the spotlight. "You don't have to if you don't want to. It's okay."

Lexi looked at her father, then her friend. "Are you kidding? Let me at it! Who wants to hear Katy Perry's 'Roar'?" She jumped onto the stage set up in the backyard and grabbed the microphone. When she was finished performing not one, but two Katy Perry tracks ("Firework" was her encore), Lexi took a bow.

"Well, somebody certainly came out of her shell," Mr. Poole said. "I'm proud of you."

"Cupcakes and karaoke." Lexi winked at him. "Who could ask for anything more?"

Matcha-macallit
Green Tea Cupcakes

Green Tea Cupcakes

Makes 12 cupcakes

> 6 ounces (1 stick plus two tablespoons) unsalted butter, room temperature
>
> 1½ cups sugar
>
> 2 eggs
>
> ⅔ cup milk
>
> ½ teaspoon vanilla extract
>
> 2 cups all-purpose flour
>
> 2 tablespoons green tea (matcha powder)
>
> ½ tablespoon baking powder

1. Preheat the oven to 350°F. Line a muffin pan with cupcake liners.

2. In the bowl of an electric mixer, beat the butter on medium speed until it's creamy. Beat in the sugar, a little at a time, until the mixture turns fluffy.

3. Add the eggs, one at a time, beating well.

4. Beat in the milk and vanilla until combined.

5. In a separate bowl, mix together the flour, green tea powder, and baking powder. Add these dry ingredients to the liquid mixture slowly and on low speed until combined. Then beat on medium speed for about a minute more until smooth.

6. Fill the liners with the batter, about two-thirds full.

7. Bake for about twenty-five minutes or until a toothpick inserted into the center of a cupcake comes out clean.

8. Cool the cupcakes for at least fifteen minutes, then frost and top them with your fave decorations—or fondant shaped like sushi, à la PLC!

Green Tea Buttercream Frosting

2 tablespoons half-and-half

1 tablespoon green tea (matcha) powder

½ cup (1 stick) unsalted butter (preferably Plugrá), room temperature

3 cups confectioners' sugar

1. In a small bowl, mix the half-and-half and green tea powder to form a paste.
2. In the bowl of an electric mixer, beat the butter until it's creamy. Scrape down the sides of the bowl.
3. Add the sugar, one cup at a time on medium speed, and the green tea paste. Beat until the frosting is light and smooth—and a gorgeous, light-green color!

Pretty as a Pageant Winner
Pink Velvet Cupcakes

Pink Velvet Cupcakes

Makes 12 cupcakes

½ cup sugar

½ cup unsalted butter (1 stick), room temperature

2 eggs

1 teaspoon vanilla

1¼ cups all-purpose flour

¾ teaspoon baking powder

¼ teaspoon baking soda

¼ teaspoon salt

½ cup buttermilk, room temperature

1/8 teaspoon pink gel food coloring (use more for a
    deeper pink color)

1. Preheat the oven to 350°F. Line a muffin pan with
   cupcake liners. For these pink velvets, we like pink
   liners or shiny metallic ones.

2. In the bowl of a mixer, cream the sugar and butter until light and fluffy. Add the eggs, one at a time, beating well. Beat in vanilla.

3. In a separate large mixing bowl, whisk together the flour, baking powder, baking soda, and salt.

4. Add half the dry ingredients to the creamed mixture with half the buttermilk. Finish by adding the rest of the dry ingredient mixture and then the rest of the buttermilk, beating well after each. Beat well after each addition, but be careful not to overbeat! The mixture should be smooth but not soupy.

5. Finally, add the food coloring till you achieve the perfect shade of pink for your cupcakes. The gel coloring is pretty concentrated, so use a very small amount for a paler pink.

6. Fill each cupcake liner two-thirds full with batter. Bake approximately twenty-five minutes or until a toothpick inserted in the center of a cupcake comes out clean.

To make the special, surprise star cake within a cupcake:

1. Follow the above cake recipe, leaving out the food coloring (or you can use another color like pur-

ple for a colored star), and pour the batter into a greased, nonstick nine-inch round cake pan. Bake for about 20 minutes or until a toothpick inserted in the center of the cake comes out clean.

2. When the cake is done, allow it to cool. Then use a small, 2-inch star-shaped cookie cutter to cut out mini stars. Remove and set aside twelve of them.

3. Spoon a tablespoon of the pink velvet batter into each liner. Put one star into each liner, and press it point down into the batter. Spoon the batter on either side of the star and over the top of the star so it is completely covered. (The liner should be approximately two-thirds full with batter.)

4. Bake approximately twenty-five minutes, or until the top of the cupcake springs back when you push gently on it. (Careful! It will be hot, so have a grown-up check for you.) Checking with a toothpick won't work well since the baked star is in the middle!

5. Allow the cupcakes to cool completely before frosting. When you bite one, you'll see stars!

White Chocolate Buttercream Frosting

1 (4-ounce) white chocolate baking bar

1/3 cup heavy cream

1 cup butter (2 sticks), room temperature

1 (2-pound) package confectioners' sugar

1/4 cup heavy cream

2 teaspoons vanilla extract

Directions

1. Break the white chocolate bar into small squares and place them in a microwave-safe bowl. Add 1/3 cup heavy cream, and microwave on medium (50 percent power) for about thirty seconds. Stir the mixture and put it back in the microwave for another thirty seconds, until the chocolate is melted and smooth. Do not overcook! Once the chocolate is melted, allow it to cool for approximately twenty minutes at room temperature.

2. In the bowl of an electric mixer, beat butter at medium speed until it is creamy.

3. Slowly add in the sugar and the remaining heavy cream (1/4 cup), beating at low speed until blended.

Beat in chocolate mixture and vanilla until light and fluffy.

4. Frost your cooled cupcakes with a knife, spatula, or a piping bag. Decorate them with whatever you like: sprinkles, chips, candy, or fondant stars like Lexi's!

Harleigh's Pumpkin Pie Cupcakes

Pumpkin Pie Cupcakes

Makes 12 cupcakes

   1 (15-ounce) can of pumpkin

   ½ cup sugar

   ¼ cup brown sugar

   2 eggs

   ¾ cup condensed milk (sweetened)

   ¾ cup all-purpose flour

   1 teaspoon pumpkin pie spice

   ¼ teaspoon baking powder

   1 teaspoon ground cinnamon

   ¾ teaspoon salt

   ¼ teaspoon baking soda

1. Preheat the oven to 350°F. Line a muffin pan with paper cupcake liners.

2. In the large bowl of a mixer, mix the pumpkin, sugar,

brown sugar, eggs, and condensed milk together until combined.

3. Add the flour, pumpkin pie spice, baking powder, cinnamon, salt, and baking soda, and mix until well combined.

4. Fill the liners two-thirds full with batter. Bake about twenty-five minutes, or until a toothpick inserted in the center of a cupcake comes out clean. Cool the cupcakes fifteen minutes before frosting them.

Cinnamon Buttercream Frosting

½ cup butter (1 stick), room temperature

3¾ cups confectioners' sugar

3 tablespoons milk

1 teaspoon cinnamon

1 teaspoon vanilla extract

1. In the bowl of an electric mixer, beat the butter at medium speed until creamy.

2. Slowly add in the sugar, one cup at a time, beating on low.

3. Add the milk, cinnamon, and vanilla. Beat on medium for about two minutes until frosting is smooth

and light. If it's too thick, you can add 1 tablespoon more of milk.

Magnolia has always been one of my fave cupcakeries in NYC. I never cease to be wowed by how pretty their cupcakes are. They have mastered the art of frosting with an offset spatula (kind of like a long, flat metal paddle). No matter what the holiday or occasion, Magnolia creates cupcakes that are mini works of art. I'm also a big fan of their pies, muffins, and banana pudding! You can imagine how excited I was to meet Bobbie and ask her to tell me all about her amazing job. We talked all things cupcake…

Carrie: How did you get started in cupcakes? Were you always into baking as a kid?

Bobbie: I started baking with my mother, grandmother, and even my great-grandmother when I was a little girl. I have always loved baking something—cake, bread, pies, and cookies for friends, family, and neighbors. It seemed to be a natural transition to make this a career.

Carrie: Why are cupcakes so popular? And how did Magnolia start making them?

Bobbie: We have all grown up with cupcakes as part of the American culture. At Magnolia Bakery they became an extension of a product line based on cakes. A little leftover batter one day turned into an entire product line because people wanted it.

Carrie: What makes Magnolia Bakery so special?

Bobbie: Everything! The moment you walk into our stores, you are transported by the smells and the activity of baking in the store. Watching our cake and cupcake icers is part theater and part production. It's a sensory experience from the minute you walk in to when you taste the perfect confection.

Carrie: What are your fave Magnolia flavors? What are the most popular ones in the stores?

Bobbie: Our bestselling cupcake is always the vanilla cake with vanilla buttercream. I think people just love a classic cupcake. For me, I love all things peanut butter. At Magnolia Bakery we serve the most amazing peanut-butter-and-jelly cupcake. I could eat the peanut-butter buttercream by the cupful, it's so good.

Carrie: How do you come up with your ideas for new cupcakes? What have been some really fun ones?

Bobbie: I usually think about what the season offers. For example, we recently did a harvest apple cupcake for October. The recipe was based on our most popular muffin, the apple walnut muffin. When I thought about what everyone loves about this muffin, I created a cupcake using the same flavor profile of tart apples and cranberries with the warm spice combination of an apple pie. Perfection!

Carrie: You've judged *The Next Great Baker* for Cake Boss—I know, because I was one of the kids helping judge that episode! In your opinion, what makes a great cake?

Bobbie: I had so much fun as a judge on *The Next Great Baker*. The bakers and decorators that competed on the show came with a huge variation in skill levels. Some were better bakers, and some were better at decorating with no baking skill at all. For me, a cake is all about taste and texture, but of course you want the cake to be beautiful. In the end, you are eating a cake after all. To make the amazing sculptural cakes for the show, you have to use fondant and other ingredients that may not taste great but provide the structure you need for a large cake.

Carrie: Magnolia has a really great way of frosting its cupcakes. Can you share your secret?

Bobbie: There really are no secrets to the famous Magnolia swirl. It takes hours to learn the technique, which is a ten-step process. The right type of buttercream, the right texture, and of course, the right tools will set you on the right path. Then it's just hours of practice. I compare our process to Olympic training. We make it look easy in the end because we are fast and consistent, but there are hours of practice behind what we make look so easy.

Carrie: How many Magnolia stores are there?

Bobbie: There are five in NYC, one in Chicago, and one in LA. We have eight stores in the Middle East, and one each in Japan, Moscow, and Mexico City. In 2015 we have about another eighteen stores planned to open.

Carrie: How can we get some of those Magnolia recipes to bake at home? Do you have a cookbook?

Bobbie: The original owner of Magnolia Bakery, Allysa Torrey, has three books. The most recent one is called *The Complete Magnolia Bakery Cookbook*. You can find it at www.magnoliabakery.com or your favorite bookstore.

Carrie: Thanks so much, Bobbie!

Me, my camp bestie Ally, and Magnolia Bakery's Bobbie Lloyd

Bobbie Lloyd

Acknowledgments

Many thanks to our family, the Berks, Saps, and Kahns! Jason: you always wanted a boy to be in PLC... We gave you Herbie! Brad: our new robotics whiz of an advisor was inspired by you (minus the red hair!).

Many thanks to Carrie's TDS teachers and friends! Ms. McNally, Ms. Murphy, Ms. Rathbone, Mr. Sullivan, Mr. Danenburg: hope you get a kick out of your "names" in the book ;-) What a great year it's been in seventh grade!

To our good friends at East Coast USA Pageants/East Coast Starz (http://eastcoaststarz.com/) for making Carrie feel beautiful and confident. You helped her find her voice, just like Lexi! You were our first pageant and will always have a special place in our hearts. Lauren Handler, Stacie Fitzgerald, Elizabeth Percy, and Mr. Tim, hugs and sprinkles! Now you've all been immortalized in the Cupcake Club! Lilly and Paige: you are the sweetest! We'll be seeing you starring on Broadway and the big screen one day soon...

Kim Gravel and the gang at Pageant Place (Amy, Allisyn, Miss Jo): You have the biggest hearts and the biggest crowns! We love you all and *Kim of Queens*. Kim, you are *ah-may-zing*. There is nothing you can't do! We believe in you!

Hannah Stark: Carrie is so glad she found her "sister." Harleigh is for you! You are such an incredible, caring, loving, brilliant, sweet soul. We know your Barbie Mama is proud of you. We are too! Your faith is incredible.

Amaryllis "Lilly" Rodriguez: our fave *American Idol* contender, pageant queen, and coach. You are such a star! Can we say we knew you when…?

To Jennifer Curfman: We promised and here it is—your very own shout-out and your very own character (Miss Jen)! You have done the most amazing job in bringing the girls of PLC to life onstage at Vital! We can't thank you enough! XO

Christina Jackson and Meghan Ross: We had to put Meredith and Lexi head-to-head for you guys! Hope you loved their rematch as much as we did. We just need to picture you two onstage and the characters write themselves!

To the gang at Sourcebooks, Steve Geck, Kate Prosswimmer, Elizabeth Boyer: thanks for making every book such a fun and fabulous experience. We hope Cupcake Club never ends!

Katherine Latshaw at Folio: wish we could give you a lifetime supply of cupcakes for all your hard work and encouragement. Thanks as always…

About the Authors

Sheryl Berk is the *New York Times* bestselling co-author of *Soul Surfer*. An entertainment editor and journalist, she has written dozens of books with celebrities including Britney Spears, Jenna Ushkowitz, and Zendaya. Her daughter, Carrie Berk, is a renowned cupcake connoisseur and blogger (www.facebook.com/PLCCupcakeClub; www.carriescupcakecritique.shutterfly.com; Instagram @) with over 105K followers at the tender young age of 12! Carrie cooked up the idea for the Cupcake Club series while in second grade. To date, they have written seven books together (with many more in the works!). *Peace, Love, and Cupcakes* had its world premiere as a delicious new musical at New York City's Vital Theatre in 2014. The Berk ladies are also hard at work on a new series, The Fashion Academy, due out on shelves Spring 2015. Stay tuned!

Peace and Love and CUPCAKES

Meet Kylie Carson.

She's a fourth grader with a big problem. How will she make friends at her new school? Should she tell her classmates she loves monster movies? Forget it. Play the part of a turnip in the school play? Disaster! Then Kylie comes up with a delicious idea: What if she starts a cupcake club?

Soon Kylie's club is spinning out tasty treats with the help of her fellow bakers and new friends. But when Meredith tries to sabotage the girls' big cupcake party, will it be the end of the cupcake club?

Book
1

Recipe For Trouble

Meet Lexi Poole.

To Lexi, a new school year means back to baking with her BFFs in the cupcake club. But the club president, Kylie, is mixing things up by inviting new members. And Lexi is in for a not-so-sweet surprise when she is cast in the school's production of *Romeo and Juliet*. If only she could be as confident onstage as she is in the kitchen. The icing on the cake: her secret crush is playing Romeo. Sounds like a recipe for trouble!

Can the girls' friendship stand the heat, or will the cupcake club go up in smoke?

Book

2

Winner Bakes All

$\mathcal{M}$eet Sadie.

When she's not mixing it up on the basketball court, she's mixing the perfect batter with her friends in the cupcake club. Sadie's definitely no stranger to competition, but the oven mitts are off when the club is chosen to appear on *Battle of the Bakers*, the ultimate cupcake competition on TV. If the girls want a taste of sweet victory, they'll have to beat the very best bakers. But the real battle happens off camera when the club's baking business starts losing money. Long recipe short, no money for icing and sprinkles means no cupcake club.

With the clock ticking and the cameras rolling, will the club and their cupcakes rise to the occasion?

Book
3

Icing on the Cake

$\mathcal{M}$eet Jenna.

She's the cupcake club's official taste tester, but the past few weeks have not been so sweet. Her mom just got engaged to Leo—who Jenna is sure is not "The One"—and Peace, Love, and Cupcakes has to bake the wedding cake. Jenna is ready to throw in the towel, especially when she hears the wedding will be in Las Vegas on Easter weekend, one of the most important holidays for the club's business!

Can Jenna and her friends handle their busy orders—and the Elvis impersonators—or will they have a cupcake meltdown?

Book
4

Baby Cakes

$\mathcal{M}$eet Delaney.

New cupcake club member Delaney is shocked to find out her mom is expecting twins! When her parents first tell her, the practical joker thinks they must be pulling her leg. For ten years she's had her parents—and her room—all to herself. She LIKED being an only child. But now she's going to be a big sis.

The girls of Peace, Love, and Cupcakes get together to bake cupcakes and discover Delaney is worried about what kind of a big sister she will be. She's never even babysat before! But her cupcake club friends rally to her side for a crash course in Big Sister 101.

Book
5

Royal Icing

$\mathscr{M}$eet Kylie.

As the founder and president of Peace, Love, and Cupcakes, Kylie's kept the club going through all kinds of sticky situations. But when PLC's advisor surprises the group with an impromptu trip to London, the rest of the group jumps on board—without even asking Kylie. All of sudden, Kylie's noticing the club doesn't need their president nearly as much as they used to. To top it off, the girls get an order for two thousand cupcakes from Lady Wakefield of Wilshire herself—to be presented in the shape of the London Bridge! Talk about a royal challenge...

Can Kylie figure out her place in the club in time to prevent their London Bridge—and PLC—from falling down?

Book
6

Here's a sneak peek of the
next Cupcake Club book

Cupcake
Countdown

Okay, this is one hula-larious cupcake order!" Jenna held up her phone and showed an email to her fellow cupcake clubbers. "It's for a surprise thirtieth birthday party this weekend with a Hawaiian luau theme.

"Ooh! I can pipe those pretty Hawaiian flowers," Lexi said, grabbing the phone out of her hand to read the details. "You know, white, pink, and yellow plumeria."

"I think we should use a decorating tip and make green grass icing," Delaney suggested. "Like those grass skirts the hula girls wear." She snatched Sadie's fringed scarf from around her neck and tied it around her waist. "Aloha...OY! Aloha...OY!" She sang and swayed around Kylie's kitchen, waving her arms in the air.

"Aloha, *ay dios mío!*" Jenna quipped. "You look like you're swatting mosquitos!"

"I believe it's 'Aloha O'e,'" Herbie pointed out. "It means 'farewell to thee.'"

"And you know this because you are a human search engine of weird facts?" Kylie asked. Her new advisor was a bit of a know-it-all—and she couldn't help calling him out on it.

Herbie shook his head. "I know this because I've seen Disney's *Lilo and Stitch* a dozen times. Did I mention that I love animated movies as much as monster ones?"

"I saw that movie too!" Delaney weighed in. "That's the one where the little Hawaiian girl adopts a puppy who turns out to actually be an extraterrestrial?"

"Precisely," Herbie replied. "A classic."

"I'm all for creatures from outer space," Kylie said, "but this email says the birthday boy is a lifeguard who works at Todd's Point Beach in the summer. I don't think aliens say sand and surf, do you?"

"What if we sprinkled blue frosting with something that looked like sand?" Lexi piped up. "Like crushed graham crackers."

"We could top that with one of those little drink umbrellas," Delaney jumped in. "That says beachy."

"And a maraschino cherry would look just like a beach ball," Sadie added.

Jenna smacked her lips together. "The flavors could be

very Hawaiian: pineapple coconut or passion fruit—which is known as lilikoi in Hawaii, FYI."

Kylie climbed up on a step stool and rummaged through her mom's pantry shelves. "I know I saw some cans of crushed pineapple in here," she said. "We used it for that pineapple upside down cupcake order a few weeks ago."

"Toss me down some shredded coconut while you're at it," Jenna said. "And some brown sugar and cream of coconut too. We can do a test batch of the pineapple coconut ones tonight and pick up the rest of the ingredients tomorrow."

"Hey, Lanie. Luau's over." Lexi snapped her fingers. "I need help making the frosting and filling the piping bags.

"Aw, you guys are no fun," Delaney said, taking off her makeshift hula skirt and handing it back to Sadie. "I think it would be awesome to go to a luau."

Kylie knew her theatrical friend could never resist an opportunity to perform—and she had a great idea how to make this cupcake order extra-special. "You know what would be fun? Delivering these cupcakes wearing Hawaiian hula costumes," she suggested.

"My mom could sew them," Jenna volunteered. "No problema. I'm thinking some really loud Hawaiian-print halter tops, silk flower leis, and grass skirts."

Herbie held up his hand in protest. "Oh, no! I draw the line at wearing a coconut shell bikini."

"You're off the hook, Herbie," Kylie assured him, trying not to crack up. "You can drive us to the country club where they're having the party, but we'll do the actual hula entrance and cupcake hand-off."

"Phew!" Herbie mopped his brow with the back of his sleeve. "I'd be happy, however, to accompany you on the ukulele for your presentation."

Jenna rolled her eyes. "You play the ukulele? Seriously?"

"I've been known to dabble," Herbie answered.

"Sand…hula skirts…Hawaiian flavors, Herbie's ukulele," Kylie jotted down a list. "Are we leaving anything out?

"Hello? The Big 3-0!" Lexi reminded her. "It's a thirtieth birthday party. How do we represent that?"

"We could use thirty ingredients in each cupcake!" Delaney piped up.

"And we could be up all night baking!" Jenna corrected her. "That's a whole lotta ingredients to pack in one tiny cupcake."

"I get fifteen or sixteen max," Kylie said, listing the

sugar, butter, eggs, milk, flour, and all the rest of the necessary fruits and spices on a sheet of paper. "Nice try, Lanie."

"What about arranging the cupcakes so they form the numbers three and zero?" Lexi said, using her colored pencils to whip up a quick sketch.

"Anything with math and numbers scares me," Sadie said, covering her eyes.

"No—it's good! Really good!" Kylie patted her friend on the back. "We could build a wooden sandbox, fill it with our cookie crumb sand, and arrange the cupcakes to form a thirty in it."

"My dad can build it for us," Sadie assured them. "As long as you promise there are no algebra equations involved."

Lexi crossed her fingers over her heart. "Promise!"

"Then it's a plan," Kylie said, shutting the cover to her Peace, Love, and Cupcakes club binder. "And a pretty cool one at that!"